~~YAS~~

ACPL ITEM

P9-EDX-829

SEVEN

WEEK 7:
REDEMPTION

Scott Wallens

PUFFIN BOOKS

All quoted materials in this work were created by the author.
Any resemblance to existing works is accidental.

Redemption

Puffin Books
Published by the Penguin Group
Penguin Putnam Books for Young Readers,
345 Hudson Street, New York, New York 10014, U.S.A.
Penguin Books Ltd, 80 Strand, London WC2R 0RL, England
Penguin Books Australia Ltd, Ringwood, Victoria, Australia
Penguin Books Canada Ltd, 10 Alcorn Avenue, Toronto, Ontario, Canada M4V 3B2
Penguin Books (N.Z.) Ltd, 182-190 Wairau Road, Auckland 10, New Zealand

Penguin Books Ltd, Registered Offices: Harmondsworth, Middlesex, England

Published by Puffin Books,
a division of Penguin Putnam Books for Young Readers, 2002

1 3 5 7 9 10 8 6 4 2

Copyright © 2002 17th Street Productions, an Alloy, Inc. company
All rights reserved

Front cover photography copyright © 2001 Steve Belkowitz/FPG
Back cover photography copyright (top to bottom) Stewart Cohen/Stone,
David Roth/Stone, David Rinella, Steve Belkowitz/FPG, Karan Kapoor/Stone,
David Lees/FPG, Mary-Arthur Johnson/FPG

Produced by 17th Street Productions,
an Alloy, Inc. company
151 West 26th Street
New York, NY 10001

17th Street Productions and associated logos
are trademarks and/or registered trademarks of Alloy, Inc.

ISBN 0-14-230104-3

Printed in the United States of America

Except in the United States of America, this book is sold subject to the condition
that it shall not, by way of trade or otherwise, be lent, re-sold, hired out, or otherwise
circulated without the publisher's prior consent in any form of binding or cover other
than that in which it is published and without a similar condition including
this condition being imposed on the subsequent purchaser.

THIS SERIES IS DEDICATED TO
THE MEMORY OF BLAKE WALLENS,
BELOVED HUSBAND AND FRIEND.

4/16/1970–9/11/2001

CHAPTER ONE

Peter Davis pulls his wool scarf up to cover his nose and huddles down farther in his wheelchair as his father pushes him through the packed parking lot at IHOP. It's a frigid Saturday morning, but most of the wind is blocked from behind by his dad, and when Peter gets himself in just the right position—mouth covered, hat pulled down—he can barely tell it's winter.

"Oh, look! There are the Millers!" his mother exclaims.

Peter's suddenly as alert as a dog on its way to the vet. The Millers. As in Meena Miller?

Then he spots her. Meena is walking up the steps directly across from the ramp with her parents. They all look haggard. Exhausted. All cried out. But somehow Meena also looks more at ease than he's seen her in weeks. And why not? She'd unloaded her deepest darkest secret onto her parents' shoulders—with Peter by her side. Now she has her mom and dad to help her get through it. From the sizable bags under their eyes, that's exactly what they're doing.

1

Both families arrive in front of the IHOP door at the same moment. Peter locks eyes with Meena. She gives him a small smile that lets him know she's doing okay.

"Ethan, Jackie," Peter's father says with a smile and a nod. He keeps his hands on the wheelchair. Mr. Davis has never been the best with social interaction.

"Good morning, Pete, Peter, Laura," Meena's father says with a tired smile. His eyes linger on Peter for a moment and Peter knows the man is wondering whether he has shared the Millers' family drama with his parents. Peter just looks back, his green eyes trying to convey the message—he hasn't said a word to anyone.

"Allow me," Mr. Miller says, pulling the door open.

"Thank you," Peter's father responds as he maneuvers Peter's chair over the threshold and into the bustling restaurant.

Peter's dad parks him next to the wall, away from the clutches of people waiting for tables, and asks the hostess for two tables—one in their name and another in the Millers' name.

"That'll be about fifteen minutes!" the bubbly, checkered-dress-wearing woman trills. She glances over the little multicultural group, and her smile falters just a touch as she tries to figure out who's with whom. Peter's shoulders tense, but he tries to give her the benefit of the doubt. A black kid with green eyes, a white mom, and a black dad. An Asian girl with two Irish-looking parents. It could confuse anyone. But even so, it's none of her business.

"We'd like a table by the window, if possible," Mr. Miller says in a kind but firm voice, telling the woman to go away. She grins again and does just that.

"So, Pete, how've you been?" Mr. Miller asks, turning to Peter's father. As the two moms then launch into a standard conversation about just how fattening an IHOP breakfast actually is, Meena inches her way over to Peter. By the time she gets there, Peter's heart is pounding.

"So . . . how'd it go after I left?" he asks, darting a glance at her parents.

Meena takes a deep breath. "They're okay now, I think," she says. "We were up so late talking. . . ." She reaches out and toys with the edge of one of the menus stacked on a counter next to her. "I told them pretty much everything," she adds. "They said they needed to know so they could tell the police."

Everything, Peter thinks. *She had to tell them everything.* Peter himself doesn't know the whole story of what happened to Meena. He's not sure he wants to know. His imagination has done a vivid enough job of conjuring awful details. He's afraid that if he knew exactly what happened, he might not be able to handle it.

Meena looks at Peter, her dark eyes clearly pained. "My mom actually had to throw herself in front of the door to stop my father from going over to the Claytons' new place and kicking the crap out of Steven."

I know the feeling, Peter thinks.

A smirk twists onto Meena's face but falls away quickly as if she's ashamed of the momentary lapse.

"You wanted him to, didn't you?" Peter says.

"I guess part of me did, yeah," Meena replies. "I think I was just glad he was so . . . moved."

"Well, what did you expect?" Peter asks, reaching out and touching her fingers with his. "They're your parents. I wanted to pound the guy and we're not even related."

Meena laughs and shakes her hair back from her face. "Thanks, Peter," she says. "I don't know where I'd be right now if it wasn't for you."

Peter's skin warms from her comment, but he does his best to be cool. "And really, there's no better place to be than IHOP," he jokes.

"Would you believe I'm actually hungry this morning?" Meena says, pulling her fingers away. Peter can't help feeling the absence of her touch. Still, she maintained contact longer than she ever had before. That's something. "We still have to figure out what we're gonna do next," she adds.

Peter's palms start to sweat. He wants to do something here, but he's not sure if it's the time. He's not sure he could handle the rejection even though he knows it would probably have nothing to do with him. But maybe she'll say yes. He swallows back his fear.

"Listen . . . if you need a break . . . you know, from everything," he begins awkwardly. "We could go to a movie tonight or something. If you're up to it."

The seconds before she answers are some of the most torturous his heart has ever experienced. He wants the words back. Wants it all back. Wishes he'd never said yes to this stupid IHOP run in the first place. And then Meena smiles.

"Do you know how long it's been since I've seen a movie?" she asks.

"Too long?" Peter suggests.

"Yeah. Let's do it," Meena says with a nod. "But we should go to an early one. I'm not sure how long I'm going to be able to keep my eyes open."

"It's a plan," Peter says. *A plan. Meena and I have a plan.* With no decisions to be made about telling or not telling, doing or not doing. It's just a plan. Almost a date. And after he makes this realization, he can't stop smiling.

• • •

The moment Karyn Aufiero hears her bedroom door open, she turns on her side, pulls her comforter up over her head, and squeezes her eyes shut. She does not want to get up. That would mean starting a new day, which would mean yesterday is over. And that is not acceptable.

"Karyn, are you ever getting out of bed?" her mother asks from somewhere outside the cocoon.

"No," Karyn whimpers.

What's her mother doing in here, anyway? She had a date last night. Came home late. Karyn dimly recalls half opening her eyes at 2:37 A.M. after hearing the front door close. So her mother's back at it. Back into the dating

5

scene. She'd managed to stay away from men for one whole week. Whoopee.

Why isn't she still passed out in her room with some random guy? Karyn wonders, letting a touch of bitterness seep into her contentment.

Suddenly the comforter is pulled back and the light from her overhead lamp stings her eyes. Her mother hovers over her, gazing down at Karyn with a sympathetic but stern expression.

She's already showered. This is a new and interesting development.

"You can't mope about T. J. for the rest of your life," her mother says, hands on hips.

Karyn almost laughs. She is *so* not moping about T. J. Frasier. She should be, after breaking his heart the way she did, but she's not.

Karyn couldn't mope if she tried. In fact, her mood this morning is quite giddy—so far. And it will stay that way as long as she can lie here and daydream about Reed and the amazing, romantic kiss they shared last night. But to explain that to her mother would take way too much effort.

I'm not moping about T. J., Mom. Actually, I'm fantasizing about his little brother. . . .

"Come on, Mom," Karyn says, pulling the comforter back up under her chin. "I don't have a game today. I want to sleep in."

"All right," Karyn's mother says with a sigh. "But you

have to clean out your closet. I'm going to the Salvation Army this afternoon and it's long overdue."

Karyn rolls onto her back and takes a good look at her mother. Her hair is back in a ponytail and she's not wearing any makeup. "What happened? Did you have a bad date last night?"

Her mother blinks. Crosses her arms over her chest. "Actually, it was a lovely date," she says. "Thanks for asking in such a sarcastic tone."

Karyn blushes slightly—guiltily. "Sorry," she says. "It's just that you're always in chore mode the day after a bad date. If you'd had a good date, you'd still be . . ."

"In bed?" her mother says, flinching. She glances away for a second, but not fast enough for Karyn to miss seeing the pain in her eyes. Then she takes a deep breath and returns her gaze to Karyn. "Well, maybe this is the new me," she says. "And the new me is telling you not to waste the whole day in here."

"Fine," Karyn says, rolling her eyes and turning onto her side again. But she can't help a small smile.

Taking the hint, Karyn's mother grabs Karyn's overflowing hamper and walks out, shutting the door behind her. Karyn stares at the door for a moment, letting what her mother just said sink in. *The new me.* So maybe her mom is trying. Maybe she's really trying to change her life.

How many miracles can occur in one weekend?

Karyn closes her eyes and tries to call back the images of

the night before. Reed waiting for her alone at the Falls, the romantic picnic, the kissing. But it's too late. Reality is sinking in.

You can't be with him, a little voice in her mind tells her. *There are a million reasons why you can't be with him.*

Not the smallest of which is the new development in T. J. and Reed's relationship. Last night, after all the kissing and eating and talking about themselves, Reed had told Karyn something totally out of left field. Next year, Reed will be the starting quarterback at Boston College, taking the spot from T. J. Taking away the most important thing in T. J.'s life. The most important thing aside from Karyn.

In one week, T. J. has lost the girl he loves and the starting position he's been craving his whole life. Reed is going to be the quarterback—there's no getting around that. And Karyn is proud of him and happy for him. But if Reed gets Karyn as well . . .

Karyn doesn't even want to think about how T. J. would react.

Exhaling loudly, Karyn flings off her comforter. Life is just not fair.

With Reed, she could have everything. He's her best friend. And when he kisses her, it's like she knows she's kissing the one person she's meant to be with. He makes her happy. He makes her feel safe. He knows the real her—everything about her—and he still wants her. Can she really give that up to spare T. J.'s feelings?

But it's not just T. J. standing in the way, a little voice in Karyn's head reminds her.

"You're supposed to be all independent now," Karyn says aloud, both hands gripping her comforter—bunching it into little balls in her fists. "You decided. No guys. Not for a while."

Why is Reed doing this to her? Why now? Now that she's decided to see how she fares without a guy? To see if she can stand on her own. *Now* the love of her life decides to declare his feelings for her? Is this some kind of sick joke?

"This is stupid," Karyn says aloud, her eyes popping open again. "I'm just going to go out with him. I can't miss this chance."

But as determined as she sounds, a twinge of guilt immediately starts nagging at the back of her mind. It doesn't matter how much she wants Reed. She can't just jump into another relationship or she'll never have time to figure out who she really is, to prove to herself that she *can* be okay alone. That she's not destined to end up like her mom.

Karyn groans loudly, shoving herself out of bed so fast, she gives herself a head rush. Sometimes her own thoughts sound so much like articles right out of women's magazines, she feels like she can tear the pages from her head. Is she doing the right thing, or is she just reading too much propaganda?

She stalks over to her closet and yanks down on the chain to turn on the light. Shaking with irritation, she starts to pull out clothing at random, tossing sweaters, shirts, skirts, pants on the floor behind her.

"How am I supposed to know what's best for me when everybody wants me to do something different?" she mutters, tearing a T-shirt she hasn't worn since picture day, freshman year, off a shelf.

Reed looked so psyched and petrified the night before, it nearly breaks her heart to think of him. She wants him so much, she actually aches inside. But then she hears her mother's voice. Remembers how proud she was when Karyn told her she was going to be alone for a little while.

Maybe that's the right path. Maybe she just has to be strong and tell Reed they aren't going to be together. Not now, anyway.

Karyn pulls a skirt from its hanger and tosses it on the floor, then pauses to look at what she's done. She doesn't want to get rid of these things. What's wrong with her?

Suddenly all she can think about is crawling back under the covers. She steps over the mess it took her about two minutes to make and slides across her sheets, pulling the comforter up over her head once more.

Maybe she'll just sleep for a little while longer. At least when she's asleep, she can't confuse herself.

• • •

By the time Reed Frasier finally pries his eyes open on Saturday morning, he's already smiling. When he realizes why, the smile broadens. He reaches up and stretches his

10

arms into the air, then crooks them and rests his head back on his hands.

I kissed her. I finally, finally kissed her, he thinks giddily. He recalls every detail—the way the breeze lifted Karyn's long blond hair away from her face, the certainty in her blue eyes as he leaned in, the softness of her lips. He's been awake for five seconds and he's already managed to stir up things that shouldn't be stirred before breakfast.

Last night was not their first kiss. But it was the first one that felt right. The first one he initiated and hadn't pulled away from in a paralyzing mix of guilt and fear. And it was incredible.

There's a loud slam from somewhere down the hall, and Reed's heart immediately leaps into his throat. He flips over onto his side, alert and listening, his pulse racing. It's irrational, he knows this, but it's the way he always reacts to loud noises in his house. He was trained to as a child, and he's never gotten over it. Slamming and pounding always meant his father was in a rage, and if his father was in a rage, it was best to try to figure out exactly where he was. Was he getting closer? Was he coming for Reed?

More slamming. Pounding. Drawers crashing shut. It's not Reed's dad. The man has been dead for years. But Reed has a pretty good idea of who's making all the noise. And it's not a very comforting revelation.

Reed lies back on his bed and brings his hands to his head, pressing the heels of his palms into his temples. T. J., his brother, is down in his room, throwing a fit. Reed has been waiting for this. The reaction to his news last night had been far too subdued—shocked, but subdued. And now that the reality has set in, T. J. is blowing off some serious steam.

Reed knows he needs to talk to him. He has to make his brother understand. He swings his legs over the side of the bed, reaches to the floor, and picks up his sweatpants. Standing, he pulls them on over his boxers in one smooth motion and heads out into the hallway.

His heart slams against his rib cage as he creeps along the thick carpeting, getting closer and closer to the battle-worthy noises. Reed holds his breath. He's not even going to bring up Karyn. Doing that might push his brother over the edge. But he knows that having this conversation, and holding back this huge secret about T. J.'s ex, is just going to make it that much harder.

Still, he has to try. He has to fix one wound before he opens up another.

Reed reaches out a tentative hand and pushes open the door to T. J.'s bedroom. It makes a loud creak, and Reed knows his brother hears it. But T. J. doesn't stop what he's doing. He ducks into the closet and rumbling ensues. The room already looks like the Tasmanian devil came by for a fashion show. Clothes, shoes, sheets, CDs, and videotapes are strewn everywhere.

"T. J.?" Reed says, loudly enough for his brother to hear him in the depths of his closet even over all the noise.

No answer.

"T. J.?" Louder. He takes a step into the room. Nothing. The longer T. J. goes without answering, the harder Reed's heart pounds. Maybe this wasn't the best idea. . . .

There's another clatter as something falls from a shelf, then T. J. walks out of the closet, head down, deliberately looking away from Reed. His skin is red and he's sweating. He drops to the floor and half disappears under the bed. Reed can hear little grunts and a few things come flying out next to T. J.'s feet. Deflated football, jockstrap, box of baseball cards. Finally T. J. emerges, clutching a beat-up blue-and-gold football jersey. His practice jersey from Falls High.

Reed presses his teeth together as his brother pushes himself to his feet and shoves the jersey into an already jam-packed duffel bag. T. J. is obviously trying to cling to the past—to his glorious run as Falls High's football hero. He doesn't want to believe it's over. He doesn't want to believe that what Reed told him the night before is true.

That Reed is going to be the starting quarterback at Boston College next year. That his little brother is ousting him from his place on the team.

"T. J.," Reed says, much more quietly this time. "Come on. We have to talk."

T. J. zips the bag, grabs his jacket, and walks right by Reed. He never looks at him. Never says a word. He's down the stairs and out the front door before Reed can even make himself move. Moments later, he hears T. J.'s

13

car peel out into the street. Reed walks over to the railing at the top of the stairs and looks down at the shining marble floor below.

This is not good, Reed thinks, grasping the wooden railing with both hands. *This is not good at all.*

There's a clicking sound down below and Reed realizes his mother is coming toward the stairs from the foyer. His blood runs cold, but he doesn't have time to duck back into his room. When she looks up at him, she has one hand at her throat, and she seems shaken, like a couple of cops have just come to the door and told her someone has died.

"I hope you're happy," she says to Reed, her steel gaze cutting right through him.

He's so sick, he can't even respond. His brother hates him. His mother not only hates him but clearly loves his brother more. It's so obvious. It always has been. But the events of the last few weeks have done nothing but drive that point home again and again. He wants to scream at her. He wants to shake her and ask her what he ever did to make him second best.

But he knows it won't matter. So he simply turns around and goes back to his room.

• • •

"I don't think I've ever laughed so hard at a movie," Peter says as Meena holds the theater door open for him on Saturday night.

The pungent smell of movie-theater popcorn clings to

Meena as she steps out onto the cold sidewalk. She forgot how much she loves everything about going to the movies—the food, the comfy seats . . . sitting in the dark and thinking about nothing for almost two whole hours.

"I know. Me too," Meena replies, biting her bottom lip. She can't remember the last time she felt so light and almost happy. "And I didn't even think it was that funny, but when you laugh, I laugh."

"Why? Is my laugh that bad?" Peter asks as he turns his wheelchair to face her. An older man has to sidestep to keep from ramming right into him, but Peter doesn't seem to notice.

"No! No!" Meena says, buttoning up the front of her coat. "It's just . . . contagious. Didn't you notice that the people sitting around us were having a better time than everyone else? That was because of you."

Peter covers his face with his gloved hands. "Okay, just hide me," he says.

"It's no big deal. Forget I said anything," Meena says. She steps behind him, takes hold of the handles on the back of his chair, and starts to push him down the street. After a few steps, the sweet, strong scent of coffee fills her nostrils and her mouth actually starts to water. In the last few weeks, she has become addicted to coffee and there is no way she can pass up a cup that smells that good.

"Want to go in?" Peter asks, obviously noticing that Meena has stopped outside Dunkin' Donuts.

"Yeah," she says. "But I'm getting decaf. Don't let me not get decaf."

Once inside the brightly lit shop, Meena wheels Peter over to a table and goes up to the counter to order. She pays for two cups of coffee and one apple fritter and returns to the table, plopping into the seat across from him.

"So, have you talked to Holly?" Peter asks.

A dull ache fills Meena's stomach and she slumps. "I called her this afternoon," she says. Then she pauses and sips at her coffee. "I told her the truth this time." She feels ill just recalling the conversation and slumps even farther, the shoulders of her jacket almost touching her ears. "She didn't believe me until my mom got on the phone."

"You're kidding," Peter says, blinking. "She didn't believe you?"

"I think she didn't want to," Meena replies, taking a deep breath. "Can we talk about something else?"

"Sure. Sorry," Peter says. He looks away. "I'm such an idiot."

"No! It's okay!" Meena says, a pang of guilt mounting on top of her present discomfort. "I'm the one who sucked you into all this."

Peter pulls in a long breath and lets it out slowly. He looks at her out of the corner of his eye as if he's deciding whether or not to tell her something. Meena sits up a bit straighter.

"I want to tell you something that only my parents know," Peter says finally. He braces his arms against the table and turns himself in his chair to better face her. Meena leans forward, scraping her chair closer to the table.

Peter leans in as well. He lays his hands flat on the pink tabletop. "On Monday, I'm going to the doctor and they're going to run some tests," Peter says. Meena's eyes unwittingly flick to his lifeless legs. "And they're going to be able to tell me whether or not I'm ever going to walk again."

All the air in Meena's lungs flies right out of her. She didn't know there was even a possibility of him walking again. Has never even asked. When it comes down to it, she and Peter have talked of almost nothing in their short but intense relationship other than her and her problems. Meena's guilt intensifies. She's been so selfish. Yes, she's been through hell. But Peter has also been struggling with this huge, scary thing. . . .

But he's smiling. He may or may not ever walk again, and he's smiling.

"You're . . . you're kidding," Meena says, her hands clasped under the table. She leans in forward so that her face is almost touching the top of her coffee cup. "Peter, that's huge," she says.

How can he be smiling as he tells her this? Isn't he petrified? She knows she would be petrified.

"Yeah. It kind of is, I guess," Peter says, lifting one shoulder.

He's playing it cool. But why? Why play it cool with her of all people? She's trusted him with everything. She wants him to trust her back.

"Aren't you . . . worried?" Meena says tentatively. She doesn't want to make him feel hopeless, or make him feel that she thinks he's a lesser person in his chair and should therefore be scared of never getting out of it. It's so hard to tell what to say and what not to say.

But then Peter sits back, and he's still smiling. "I know it sounds weird, but I'm not," he says. "Everything has been going so well lately. . . . I just feel like it's all going to be okay. I really think it's going to be good news."

Meena feels a smile pull at her lips. It's hard not to feel confident when Peter is so sure. But still, total optimism is not in her nature. At least not anymore.

"It's great that you're so positive," Meena says, running her fingertip around and around the rim of her coffee cup. "But . . . what if it's not good news? Have you . . . I don't know . . . prepared yourself for that?"

She hazards a glance in his direction. His expression hasn't changed. He looks content. Assured. Serene. How does he do it?

"I'll be fine," Peter says. "Besides, you shouldn't be worrying about me. I just wanted to let you know what was going on. You should be taking care of yourself."

"I am," Meena says, forcing a smile. "I came out tonight, didn't I?"

Peter scoffs and picks up his coffee. "Yeah, to humor me. You didn't even like the movie, did you?"

"No! I did!" Meena says. "And if I want to humor you,

I can. If it wasn't for you, there might not be a me to take care of."

The moment the words are out of Meena's mouth, her face turns scarlet and she looks down at the table. Since when has she gotten back to being so wordy? It's been weeks since she was the say-what-she-thinks-before-she-really-thinks-about-it girl.

"I'm glad you're still here," Peter says, his voice filled with unidentifiable emotion.

Meena makes herself look at him and regrets it instantly. He has that look on his face. That dazed, intent, smoldering look. He wants to kiss her. He is, in fact, inching closer.

I want to kiss him back, Meena tells herself, her hands clasped together so tightly, her fingers are about to break. *I want to kiss him so much.*

But outweighing what she wants is the fear. The total, incredible, paralyzing fear. She can't be touched. She can't be kissed. How can she even be loved? Not after what happened to her. Not after Steven—

Suddenly Meena turns away, her stomach clenched in a million knots. Peter pulls back and Meena pretends to sneeze. It's the biggest, loudest, fakest sneeze in the history of fake sneezes. Meena considers bolting for the door.

"So anyway, I'll call you when I get back from the doctor," Peter says as if nothing has happened.

Meena pulls her coffee cup toward her, never lifting her eyes from it. "Yeah. Do that," she says, practically shaking.

She's filled with relief and gratitude toward Peter for just continuing with the conversation. He's so good, so sweet, so in tune with what she needs and wants. He's never in the past few weeks put himself ahead of her. Not once.

Meena takes a gulp of her coffee and finally looks up at Peter. He's so beautiful, really. His light brown skin, those big, startling, honest green eyes. And even in that wheelchair he looks so strong. So . . . protective. Peter would never hurt her. She knows that. She knows that as well as she knows her own name.

At that moment, Meena makes a promise to herself. She doesn't know when, she doesn't know where, but someday she's going to do it. She's going to swallow her fear and kiss Peter Davis.

CHAPTER TWO

"It's just a doorknob. Stop staring at it," Jeremy Mandile tells himself on Sunday morning. His duffel bag is in one hand. The other hand grips the strap on his backpack. He's been staring at the shiny brass doorknob on the front door of his house for at least fifteen minutes. The neighbors have to be watching. His parents are probably watching.

He's never noticed the little white streaks on the outside curve of the knob before. How did those get there, exactly? He could spend another fifteen minutes just thinking about it.

"All right. That's it," Jeremy says. He reaches out his hand, turns the doorknob, steps inside. He's in. He'd let out a sigh of relief if he wasn't still so nervous.

The moment he's inside, his golden retriever, Pablo, runs up to him, his tail wagging like mad. Jeremy crouches to scratch behind the dog's ears and get a few comforting licks on his cheeks.

"Hey, buddy! How ya been?" Jeremy says as the dog pants away happily.

When Jeremy stands again, the dog runs into the kitchen as if to announce his presence. Jeremy stands there for a moment feeling like he's coming home from a war and he's not exactly sure if everyone's going to be happy to see him. Although if he *had* been at war, everyone would be delighted to have the prodigal son return. In his present situation, that's not guaranteed. Sure, they invited him to move back, but if the nervous pounding of his heart is any indication, it's not going to be the easiest transition.

"Jeremy!"

His mother walks into the foyer with a huge, almost comical grin on her face. She's dressed in slim black pants and a nice sweater—too nice for a lazy Sunday morning. Jeremy drops his bag on the floor and looks her up and down. Are they filming an episode of Martha Stewart's show here or something?

"We held breakfast for you," she says, giving him a hug.

"Uh . . . thanks," Jeremy says, shrugging out of his varsity jacket. "You didn't have to do that."

He follows her into the kitchen and finds his father and his sister are already seated at the table—Dad reading the paper, Emily with her eyes glued to some silly teen show on the tiny TV on the counter. There's a steaming plate of banana pancakes at Jeremy's usual place. Banana pancakes, universally detested by all Mandiles except Jeremy, who only gets them on his birthday. Interesting.

"Good morning, son," his father says cheerfully as Jeremy takes his seat.

"Hi, Dad," Jeremy says, unable to hide the uncertainty in his voice.

His father folds up the sports section he's reading and hands it to Jeremy. "There's a good article on the Bills in there."

Okay, I've stepped into some kind of dimension warp, Jeremy thinks, gingerly taking the newspaper and laying it on the table next to his huge glass of orange juice. In his entire life his father has never given up the sports section before he was done with it. He has, in fact, taken it right out of Jeremy's hands many times so that he could read it first thing.

What is going on around here?

"Hey, Emily," Jeremy says, hoping to at least get some normalcy out of his sister.

"Hi!" she says brightly, looking away from the TV. "Did you want to watch something else?"

Before Jeremy can even answer, she picks up the remote and switches over to *NFL Today.* Jeremy's hands curl into fists under the table. Could they be any more obvious? He'd rather they ignore his presence than treat him like he's a guest of honor.

"I know what you're doing, and you don't have to," he says, looking down at his plate.

"What are we doing?" Emily asks with a little too much innocence.

23

"All this special treatment," Jeremy says, managing to look at his father, who quickly looks away, shifting his large, solid frame in his chair. "It's not like I've been in the hospital or something."

"Jeremy, we just wanted to welcome you home," his mother says.

"That's just it," Jeremy says, glancing up at her. "I don't want you to treat me like something's happened or like I'm different. I just . . . I just want things to go back to normal."

"Don't you think normal is a little too much to ask for?" his father says, raising his thick eyebrows.

Jeremy's face heats up and he takes a deep breath, drawing himself up straight. Apparently he'd been right to be so nervous about coming back. Apparently his father still isn't ready to see that Jeremy is the same person he's always been—even if he is out of the closet now.

"I'm going up to my room," Jeremy says, pushing his chair away from the table.

"Jeremy, your father didn't mean—"

"That wasn't meant the way it sounded," his father says, cutting his mother off.

"I know," Jeremy says, even though he knows nothing of the sort. "I'm just not hungry anymore."

He turns to leave the room, ignoring his father when he tells Jeremy to sit down and eat the meal his mother prepared for him. He can't stomach food right now. And he definitely can't stomach sitting there with his father, knowing he's looking at him so differently.

Jeremy grabs his bag and takes the stairs two at a time with Pablo at his heels. Maybe he decided to move home too quickly. Maybe he should just turn around and head right back to Reed's house. Of course, things aren't exactly tension-free in the Frasier household at the moment. But at least over there, he's not the cause.

He walks into his room and steps aside so Pablo can slip by, then closes the door and takes a look around. It feels like ages since he's been here—since he was happy and secure and unconflicted.

He sits at his desk and opens the top drawer, pulling out a picture of his family taken at Christmas last year. All four of them smiling. All four of them happy. All four of them clearly having no clue what was to come. Jeremy's heart pounds painfully as he wishes he could feel like that again. Wishes they all could.

• • •

"Thanks for coming over to help me study," Jane Scott says, leaning back against her headboard. She pulls the oversized SAT study guide up on her lap and bites her lip to keep from smiling too hard as Quinn Saunders sits down next to her.

"No problem," he says. The scent of fabric softener and shampoo fills her senses and she has to bite down a little harder.

"Is this okay?" he asks, glancing at the wide-open door. "Your mom's not going to freak if she's sees us both sitting on your bed, is she?"

"Probably," Jane says. But she wouldn't tell Quinn to get up right now if it guaranteed her a 1600 on the exam. She loves the fact that she can feel his body warmth, that his weight makes her bed sag a bit in the middle. "But her only rule was 'leave the door open,' so technically, there wouldn't be much she could say."

Of course, Jane knows there would be *plenty* her mother could and would say, but this is Quinn Saunders. In her room. Even when she'd been daydreaming about him for the last four years she'd never let herself imagine him in her *room*.

He looks down at the vocabulary book in his lap. "Okay, the best way to keep you from freaking out at the test again is to make sure you are as prepared as possible."

"Okay," Jane says, putting the larger book aside. She pulls her knees up under her chin and stares at the opposite wall, ready to be quizzed.

"*Loquacious,*" Quinn says.

"Given to fluent or excessive talk," Jane says automatically.

"*Din,*" Quinn says.

"A loud noise," Jane replies.

"*Obfuscate,*" Quinn reads.

"To make obscure," Jane says.

Quinn puts down the book and looks at her. "And you freaked out about this why?" he asks.

Jane laughs, but her stomach turns dangerously as she recalls that day in October when she had her meltdown. When she'd filled out her name, gotten the worst panic attack in the history of North America, and just run.

"It's not that I wasn't prepared," she says, looking down at her almost nonexistent fingernails. "It was all the pressure."

Quinn's expression softens and he returns his attention to the book. No questions asked. He knows exactly what she means. How long has she waited to find someone who just understands?

"How's it going?" Jane's mother asks, suddenly appearing at the door. Her hand is resting on the doorjamb and her head is peeking around the corner as if she was afraid of what she might find them doing.

"Fine," Jane says, squirming a few inches away from Quinn. As much as she didn't care a few minutes ago, the last thing she wants is to endure an embarrassing tirade in front of Quinn.

"Jane is like a walking dictionary," Quinn puts in.

"She's always had a good vocabulary," her mother says, smiling a tight smile. She moves into the doorway. Jane watches her mother's eyes travel around the room and wonders what she's looking for—why she *hasn't* said anything about the two of them being on the bed. Then her mom's gaze falls on her saxophone case—her closed saxophone case that's shoved halfway under the bed.

If she asks me if I've practiced, I'm going to lose it, Jane thinks. The temperature seems to rise as the moments slowly pass. But then, suddenly, her mother looks her in the eye.

"So you two want anything?" she asks a bit stiffly. "A snack?"

"No thanks," Jane replies, her whole body rigid.

The phone rings and Jane grabs the cordless from the table next to her bed, relieved to have a reason to move.

"Hello?" she says.

"Hello, Jane, it's your father."

More stiffness.

"Hi, Dad," Jane says, glancing at her mother. She grips the phone, expecting him to ask her how the studying is going, if she's reconsidered dropping Academic Decathlon. She braces herself for a lecture.

"May I speak to your mother?" he asks.

Jane blinks. "Uh . . . sure."

She holds the phone over Quinn's chest, toward the door. "He wants to talk to you," she tells her mother.

Taking the phone, Jane's mother quickly leaves the room. Jane can hear her muffled voice as she walks down the hall to her own bedroom and closes the door. It takes her a minute or two to process everything that has just occurred. Or just *not* occurred. No orders. No suggestions. No guilt or questions or indignation. No nothing.

Jane crosses her arms over her chest, hugging herself. Something is very not right.

"What's the matter?" Quinn asks, concern creasing his face.

"My parents," Jane says, staring at her knees. "They're not talking to me, really."

It's unbelievable. She's waited her whole life for them to stop nagging her—to just leave her alone. But now they've become completely icy and it's starting to drive her crazy. Can't her parents find some kind of middle ground between overinvolved and totally distant?

"They'll get over it," Quinn says, putting his book aside and turning toward her. He picks up her hand and laces his fingers through hers. "It just takes some people a while to adjust when their kids start to grow their own brains."

Jane laughs and the tension seems to suddenly ease away. She squeezes Quinn's hand, so glad that he's here. That she finally has someone to talk to about this.

"I think it's time for a study break," Quinn says, looking into her eyes and causing her pulse to race.

"Sounds good to me," she says. As he leans in to kiss her, her eyes flutter closed and before long, her parents, the SATs, her clubs, and her saxophone are completely forgotten.

• • •

"Danny! Dinner's ready!"

Danny Chaiken pulls his eyes away from the swirling stucco pattern in his ceiling with some effort and looks at the clock. It's seven-fifteen on Sunday night. He can't remember what he was thinking about five seconds ago.

"It's happening again," he mutters under his breath, pressing the heels of his hands into his eyes to try to clear their murkiness. In the past couple of days he's started to have these little zoning episodes again, just like he had before his therapist, Dr. Lansky, switched his medication. This is why he'd wanted off. This is why he'd *taken* himself off. And the doctor promised him it wouldn't be as bad this time, on the new combination of meds.

Danny presses his lips together and makes himself breathe before he gets too angry.

It is *better,* he tells himself. *Chill out.*

The couple of episodes he's had haven't been as bad or as long as they used to be. And they're much easier to snap out of. A couple of months ago if his mother had called him to dinner, he'd probably still be staring into space right now. Staring and daydreaming.

Pushing himself off his bed, Danny walks over to the mirror over his dresser and pushes his hands through his short spiky hair a few times. His eyes fall on a little silver gift box next to his watch and suddenly he remembers what he was thinking about before his mom called him. Cori Lerner. Of course he was thinking about Cori. What else does he ever think about? He was daydreaming about giving her her Christmas present. Her surprised reaction, the make-out session that would ensue. Cori.

Feeling a bit better, Danny grabs the little blue notebook off his desk and pulls the pen out of the spiral. He uncaps it with his teeth and turns to a fresh page.

"Sunday, December second," he mumbles through the

pen cap as he writes. "Seven P.M. Zoned out. About fifteen minutes."

He pushes the pen back into the cap in his mouth and tosses it, along with the notebook, toward his backpack on the floor. Lansky wants a journal of highs and lows and Danny's going to give it to him. He's going to make that guy adjust his meds until he gets it right.

If he can get it right.

Don't think like that, he tells himself. *Don't.*

Quelling his irritation, Danny bounds down the steps and into the kitchen, where his mother, father, and twin sisters, Abby and Jenny, are putting dishes full of food on the table. Danny walks directly to the cabinet next to the refrigerator and takes down the two orange prescription bottles inside. He feels his mother's eyes on him and shoots her a glance. She quickly looks away.

Don't, Danny tells himself, feeling the back of his neck heat up. *Don't freak out.*

"I think I'm gonna quit dance," Jenny announces, plopping into her seat. "I want to play softball this year."

"Really?" Danny's father asks as Danny struggles with the lid on one of the bottles. "Why do you . . ."

When his father trails off, Danny looks over at the table and his dad and both sisters avert their gaze.

"Because," Jenny says, blushing a bit. "Dancing's for wusses, anyway."

"Hey!" Abby protests, shooting another glance in Danny's direction.

I don't believe this, he thinks, turning his back on them again as the bottle finally, mercifully pops open. *They're all watching me. My little* sisters *are keeping an eye on me.*

He dumps a couple of the tiny pills out into his sweaty palm and glares down at them. It should be his business whether or not he takes the pills. Why do they all get to act like it somehow affects *them?*

"Danny? Do you want soda?" Abby asks from the table.

He turns around and sees that she's holding the two-liter bottle of Coke up over his glass. His eyes immediately dart to her forehead and the jagged pink scar that's healing just below her hairline. He swallows hard. That's why they get to act like it affects them. Because it does.

"I'll just get water. Thanks," he tells her.

He grabs a plastic cup out of the cabinet and shoves it under the water dispenser in the door of the fridge. His hand is shaking as the jet of water splashes into the cup. Then he slaps his hand against his open mouth, launching the pills into the back of his throat, and downs the water before he can give it another thought.

When he slams the cabinet shut again and turns to sit down at the table, the conversation starts up again.

"Well, Jen, you can play softball in the spring if you want," Danny's father says with a forced smile.

Danny drops into his chair and crosses his arms over

his chest. A million sarcastic comments flit through his mind. *Must be nice to have me under control again. . . . Do you like being wardens? . . . Why don't you just install cameras in my bedroom?*

But Danny just grabs the bowl of mashed potatoes and forces himself to keep quiet. He's got to learn to control his outbursts. He's got to learn to be more mature.

I sound like Lansky, Danny thinks, lifting the spoon and slapping some potatoes onto his plate. *Wouldn't he be ever so proud?*

"What do you think, Danny?" Abby asks, pulling his attention away from his own thoughts. "Is it cooler to dance or play softball?"

Danny looks from one pair of tiny brown eyes to the other and squelches the "*Who cares?*" that's on the tip of his tongue. They're his sisters. They're only ten. The longer he looks at them, the more he softens. The more his pent-up anger starts to dissipate.

"I think they're both cool," Danny says, handing her the bowl of potatoes.

"Yeah, but would you go out with a girl who played softball?" Abby asks, her face screwing up with disgust. Jenny scowls at her.

"Absolutely," Danny says, glancing at Jenny. "As long as she didn't try to kick my butt."

The girls laugh and Danny notices his parents exchanging a little, supposedly secret smile.

They're glad I'm acting normal, Danny realizes, a twinge of indignation squeezing his heart. But he lets it pass. He can't say he's surprised. And when it comes down to it, it's good that his family is happy. He's happy his family is happy.

He just hopes he can keep it up.

• • •

Peter wakes up with a start, his heart racing, and glances at the clock. It's only been seven minutes since the last time he woke up. Exactly the same way. Every time he dozes off, it's like an explosion goes off inside his head and he jumps awake.

"Give it up. There's no way you're falling asleep tonight," Peter mutters to himself, whipping the covers away from his body.

He picks up his legs, one at a time, and places them over the side of his bed, next to his wheelchair. Then comes the part that he hates. Bed to chair. It's never fun. He reaches out and grasps the armrests of his wheelchair and pushes himself up, using all the strength in his arms. Then he swings himself over, aiming as best he can for the seat of the chair.

His hip slams into the right armrest, jarring him, but at least it doesn't hurt. He wouldn't be able to feel it if he wanted to. He leans back and takes a deep breath, lifting each leg to place his feet into their rests.

"Well, look at the bright side," he says to himself. "After tomorrow, this thing will start to be a memory."

That's right. There's nothing to be nervous about.

Everything is going to go fine at that appointment tomorrow. He's going to walk again. He knows he is. He just wishes he could convince his subconscious of that. Because apparently that particular part of him really wants to be tense about the whole thing.

Peter takes a long, deep breath and lets it out slowly. He thinks of Meena and all she's been through. He thinks of Jane and Reed and Danny and Jeremy and Karyn. They've all come back into his life out of nowhere. They've all gone through some of the hardest moments of their lives recently. And they're all moving on. They're all going to be okay.

Peter has every reason to believe that he's next. He'll complete the circle. He's been forgiven, and soon he'll find out that he's going to come through the second-hardest moment of his life. And he's going to be okay, too.

Suddenly Peter remembers something. Something he hasn't thought of in the longest time. Something he'd buried deep in the closet in this very room—his father's former office—years ago. Just like it's been buried deep in his mind. Is it still there? Could it possibly still be there?

Peter pushes his chair over to the closet door, which is already half open as always, and shoves it open the rest of the way. The floor is a mess, and he needs to get to the back.

When his parents moved him from his old room upstairs to this more accessible room on the first floor, they never fully cleaned out the closet. Along the back wall they'd left the boxes of old receipts and tax forms. The boxes that a ten-year-old Peter used to hide the very thing he's looking for now, almost seven years later. He had tried to hide it in his own closet, but its presence had haunted him—kept him awake at night.

And now here he is, living in the same room with it once again.

Peter reaches down and moves his footrests aside, then braces his hands on his armrests and lowers himself to the floor as gently as possible. Grunting, Peter pulls one leg, then the other, straightening them out in front of him. He leans forward, bending at the waist, past the useless, lifeless legs, and starts to pull out the random crap he'd tossed in his closet when he moved in here. The stuff he didn't know what to do with.

Comic books. Dungeons & Dragons. Risk. Connect Four. A couple of handheld video games. A Walkman. A pile of T-shirts he'd kept out of deference to the memory of his middle school self, bearing the names of bands he hasn't listened to in ages.

He finally unearths his father's shoe boxes, each of them dented and crumbling, each of them neatly marked with a tax year in black ink. And there it is. Mashed into the corner under two boxes marked with years that predate Peter's birth. An old, dusty Adidas box with about a hundred rubber bands wrapped around it in every direction. Peter's heart turns over. Turns over again. Drops into his stomach and stays there. It's the same feeling he gets once a year when his father takes him to his grandmother's grave site. That's what he feels like he's looking at. A grave.

Trembling, Peter reaches out his hands. He can barely touch it. He holds his breath, stretching one finger, and finally manages to hook it under the lid. Sweat pouring down his temples, Peter pulls the box toward him and the two tax boxes tumble to the floor. At least five of the rubber bands snap as the Adidas box is dragged across the carpet. They're brittle and old, placed there by his ten-year-old hands.

This is not a good idea, a little voice in Peter's mind tells him. *This has been back here for so long for a reason. You don't want to look in there.*

But he does. He's almost salivating to get into the box.

Peter claws at the rubber bands. He finally gets them all off, gives himself one moment to stare reverently at the closed box, then lifts the lid.

There they are. Like no time has passed. Like someone winked and seven years went by. Four pictures. The first one takes his breath away.

Gingerly Peter lifts the photo from the box. He'd forgotten this one somehow. Just him and Meena. Laughing. All four hands holding one another as he and Meena bend toward the camera, about to double over from all the laughter. Peter has chocolate on his face. Meena's front teeth are crooked.

Placing the picture beside him on the floor, Peter forces himself to look at the next one. This one makes him laugh. Danny, Peter, Reed, Jeremy, and Harris all standing against the wall in the basement, arms crossed over their chests, chins lifted, scowls on their faces. Pure gangsta pose. Like they were ever going to be gangstas. Peter holds his breath and lets his eyes travel slowly over each of their faces. Until he gets to Harris.

Harris. He's seen him every night in his dreams. He's never forgotten what he looked like on that day. Peter's eyes start to sting and he puts the picture aside. Fast.

The next picture shows Jane, Karyn, and Meena. All smiling. Karyn is in the middle, looking every bit the precheerleader. Pink sweater, hair perfectly pulled back, very pretty. Jane, in a plaid jumper that Peter knows she probably hated. Meena, the tomboy, in jeans and a blue sweatshirt.

Peter puts this one with the others and picks up the last. His brow furrows. This isn't right. This isn't how he remembers it. All eight of them were there, weren't they? This was the group shot. So where's Harris? Why is he missing from the little clump of happy, birthday-hat-wearing kids?

Something in the background catches Peter's eye—a pile of colorfully wrapped presents—and it all comes rushing back to Peter. Harris wasn't supposed to be there. He was sick. His mother had called and told Peter's mother that Harris wasn't coming. But then, after this picture was taken, he'd shown up. Explained that he begged his mother to let him come so that he could give Peter his gift.

That plane. That stupid model airplane. Peter had talked about nothing else for days and Harris had gotten it for him and Harris had come to the party solely to watch Peter open it.

But Harris never got the chance.

Don't think about it. Not now, Peter tells himself. Chills run all over his body and he starts to tremble violently. He holds his breath and braces himself, making the shakes stop. *Don't think about it,* he orders himself. *It's over. Long over.*

He reaches up and drops the photograph into the pocket on the right side of his chair. For luck. It's not a symbol of something bad. It's a symbol of everything that has changed. Everything that is changing. He and his friends coming back together. It will bring him luck.

"Not that I'm going to need it," Peter tells himself firmly. "Everything is going to be fine."

CHAPTER THREE

Why is everybody *smiling at me?* Meena wonders on Monday morning as she slides sideways down the aisle between the wall and the desks in homeroom. She forces a small smile onto her own face to keep from being rude and drops into the last chair. Peter, who doesn't bother maneuvering behind a desk for the ten minutes of homeroom, has parked himself next to the wall by Meena's desk and he looks over at her . . . and smiles.

"What is with everybody today?" Meena asks, pushing her hair behind her ear.

"What do you mean?" Peter asks.

"Nothing," Meena replies, feeling it may be difficult to explain.

She looks around the room. Gemma Masters and Jeannie Chang exchange lipsticks and laugh, Keith Kleiner plays the drums on the desk with a pair of ballpoint pens, Christopher Adams hums to himself as he copies homework answers out of Shaheem Dobi's notebook.

"It's just everyone is so . . . happy," Meena says, scrunching up her face. "Why does everyone look so happy?"

"They don't look any happier than usual," Peter says with a shrug.

Meena turns toward the front of the room again, realizing that this may, in fact, be the first time she's looked up from the floor in homeroom in a very long time. She didn't even realize that Christopher had chopped his long hair off or that Jeannie had gotten her ears double pierced. Apparently, while she's been miserable and guilt ridden and introverted, the rest of the world has continued to go on in the same old way.

"How long have those plants been there?" she asks Peter, checking out the windowsill.

"Since Halloween," he says.

"Oookay," Meena says under her breath.

"So . . . any news on the home front?" Peter asks in a whisper.

Meena's heart falls into her stomach and she pulls herself closer to her desk, gripping the far edge with her hands.

"We're going to report him," she says, glancing at Peter out of the corner of her eye. "They're gonna set up a meeting for me so I can tell the police what happened."

A chill races down her back as a cheesy, outdated, but still terrifying scene flashes through her mind. She sits on one side of a steel table, a single lightbulb swinging over her head as two *Dragnet*-style cops interrogate her.

"Did you want him to kiss you?" one of them asks, leaning into the table. *"We know you did."*

Meena squeezes her eyes shut and gives her head a quick, almost imperceptible shake.

"You okay?" Peter asks.

"Yeah," Meena replies. She pulls back her hands and presses her sweaty palms into her lap. "I just . . . it's not going to be easy. Of course it's not going to be easy," she says with a scoff. "I just want it to be over."

"It will be soon," Peter says, his voice low. "You know you're doing the right thing . . . right?"

"Yeah. I do," Meena says. She pulls in a deep breath and sits up straight. Keith is now drumming to the beat of Christopher's humming and Shaheem is beat boxing into his hands. What would they think if they knew what she and Peter are talking about? Would they still have smiled at her when she walked into the room?

"And you know you can call me if you need to," Peter adds, his eyes conveying all his honesty and good intention. "Anytime."

Meena's heart warms and executes a happy little flip in her chest, blowing away her negative thoughts. Peter. She can't believe that *anyone* has that much of an effect on her heart, let alone Peter Davis. Peter, who until a few weeks ago she hadn't talked to in years. She can't remember the last time anyone made her heart flip—made her feel like her life was fine and good and worth it all just by looking at her in a certain way. But she can remember that it wasn't too long ago that she thought she'd never feel anything— at least not anything good—again.

"I know that, too," Meena says, smiling unconsciously this time.

"Okay, everyone! Settle down!" Ms. Johnson calls out from the front of the room. "We have a few announcements."

The teacher places her glasses on the end of her nose and picks up a piece of paper from her desk. As she starts to read off yearbook meeting announcements and details about class rings, Meena turns to her desk and opens her planner. The binding makes a crackling sound. She hasn't bothered to open the thing in weeks.

Okay . . . today is December. . . .

Meena flips through the pages until she gets to the second week of the month.

December . . .

She freezes and lets the pages drop open. Monday, Tuesday, Wednesday on the left page. Thursday, Friday, Saturday, and Sunday on the right. Her fingers start to shake and she clasps them under her desk again. Meena can't believe she didn't realize what week this was. What date this coming Friday will be. Each year she's hyperaware of the approach of December 7. Each day it gets closer, she's more and more tense, less able to sleep, less able to focus.

How could she have possibly forgotten about it this year?

Maybe because there's already enough psychoticness in your life at the moment, she thinks.

Her eyes cautiously dart to Peter, but he's doodling in his notebook. He hasn't noticed her planner. Hasn't noticed her reaction. It must be even harder for him, this time of year. It must be almost unbearable.

His birthday, Meena thinks sadly. *How awful it must be that it happened on his birthday. Every year when he's supposed to be celebrating, he must just be remembering. . . .*

It's not fair. It's just not fair. Meena stares at the little green seven, wishing there was something she could do to change it. But how? It's not like she can turn back time—make it so that it never happened. Make it so that none of them ever had to suffer with the terrible, nightmare-inflicting memory. There isn't a thing she can do to make it right.

But you can try, a little voice in her mind tells her. *He's done everything he can for you. Maybe it's time to return the favor.*

Meena reaches into her bag, pulls out a red pen, and uses her teeth to uncap it. She presses the pen to paper firmly and draws a big, definite star burst around the tiny green seven.

Peter deserves a great birthday. And she deserves to do something fun, too.

This year, it's going to be different. This year, December seventh is getting a whole new meaning.

• • •

Don't even look over there, Karyn tells herself as she walks into the cafeteria on Monday afternoon. She tosses

44

her long blond hair back behind her shoulders and heads directly for the table on the far right side of the room where her girlfriends are sitting. If she even *glances* left to where the guys usually sit, she knows Reed will be waiting to catch her eye. And if she catches his eye, she'll have to talk to him. And if she talks to him she'll have to—

Damn. She looked.

He looks really good, Karyn thinks as she keeps walking. He's wearing that blue hat that brings out his eyes and a turtleneck sweater that makes him look like an Abercrombie model. She keeps her eyes averted, pretending she hasn't noticed his presence, but now she can feel him coming toward her. She spots his blue-and-gold varsity jacket out of the corner of her eye. There's really no avoiding this.

"Karyn!"

She looks up at the sound of her name and steps out of the way of a couple of freshman girls who are trying to get by with their trays. Reed is smiling. His hands are stuffed in his pockets and he's flushed and clearly nervous, but he's smiling.

Then, with a start, Karyn realizes that he has no reason not to smile. Not yet, anyway. She hasn't told him. She hasn't told him that the reason she spent the whole weekend avoiding him and not returning his calls is because she was busy obsessing. Obsessing and coming to the conclusion that she can't be with him. He's ignorant. Blissfully ignorant.

"Hey," she says, looking down at the floor momentarily.

"Hey," he replies. "I was thinking . . . do you want to go out for lunch?"

No. Because then I'd be alone with you and I'd have no excuse to put off this conversation.

"I would, but I can't," Karyn says. "I promised Gemma, Jeannie, and Amy I'd hang with them today. Gemma's having a major Carlos crisis . . . you know."

It's a lie, technically. But Gemma *does* have a Carlos crisis almost every day, so there's a good chance she'll want to talk about *something*.

"Oh." Reed's freckled face falls and Karyn's heart falls with it.

She's in trouble. If her heart does *that* over his no-lunch-date disappointment, what's it going to do when she breaks his heart?

"That's cool," Reed says finally. He lifts his chin, looking all unaffected and manly. "I'll just hang with the guys, then."

It sounds nice and normal, but the air between them is anything but. It's supercharged with attraction, uncertainty, tension. As Reed turns to head back to his table, he hesitates, a question in his eyes. Karyn knows exactly what he's thinking. What are they supposed to do? Now that they've spent a romantic night together, does that mean they're a couple? Is he supposed to kiss her in parting or just walk away?

Please don't let him kiss me, Karyn thinks. *Just please don't let him kiss me.* Even though her lips are already tingling with anticipation. *No. He can't.*

"Okay, we need to talk," Karyn says quietly when the awkwardness finally becomes unbearable.

"Yeah," Reed replies, relieved. "Are you sure you don't want to have lunch?"

Karyn holds her breath. She knows she should just get this over with. But looking at Reed and his hopeful, clear blue eyes forces her to lose her nerve entirely. She's not ready.

"I really can't," she says, taking a step back. "But we will talk. *Soon.* I promise."

Then, before he can say anything and before she can look at him for another second and change her mind completely, Karyn turns and jogs over to her friends.

• • •

"Jeremy, can you come over here so I can hand this down to you?" Jeremy's dad asks on Monday afternoon.

Jeremy stands slowly, wiping his dusty hands on his jeans, and walks over to his father, who's standing on a step stool in the corner. He's helping his dad clean out his office at the halfway house and he's so intensely nervous, he might as well be helping shred files at the Pentagon. This is his first time back since the argument that changed his life. And it's the first time he has any chance of seeing Josh in weeks.

You don't even know if he's here, Jeremy reminds himself, reaching up to take the heavy box of files from his dad. *And it's not like you can ask Dad, so just chill out.*

But it's hard. He's been thinking about Josh ever since their fight. Ever since Jeremy's parents overheard them arguing

47

about their kiss and the fact that Josh had shown up at Jeremy's school, pretty much confirming to the student body that he was gay. Jeremy hasn't been back to the halfway house since that day, but as far as he knows, Josh still works here. Which means he could be in this building right now . . .

Jeremy reaches up and braces his arms under the weight of the box, but it starts to slide. He tries to right the box, but it's too late. Files smack to the floor, fanning papers and manila folders out in a jagged arc. Jeremy braces for the explosion. There isn't much his father is more obsessive about than the organization of his office.

"Uh . . . sorry," Jeremy says, looking up at his father.

His dad shakes his head and chuckles. "It's okay. We're gonna toss that stuff, anyway."

"Thank God," Jeremy says with a laugh. And just like that, the ice is broken. Jeremy feels a thousand times better, simply having laughed in his father's presence.

Then the office door opens and the air whooshes out of Jeremy's lungs. Josh stands in the open doorway. About five years pass in the space of five seconds. Neither one of them can tear their eyes away from the other.

"Hey," Josh says, blushing and glancing up at Jeremy's father, who's watching them closely.

"Hey," Jeremy replies. He finally pulls his gaze away. Somehow. He could look at those deep brown eyes for days. He'd forgotten how very deep and brown they were.

"Mr. Mandile, I was just wondering if it would be all

right if I cut out a little early today," Josh says, his eyes wandering over to Jeremy again. "I have to be at school tonight for auditions."

"Auditions?" Jeremy hears himself say.

"I'm co-directing the play," Josh replies.

"Oh . . . that's . . . cool," Jeremy says.

Cool, he hears his voice echo in his head. *I am such an inarticulate loser.*

"Sure, Josh," Jeremy's father says. "Just let Rita know before you leave."

"Thanks," Josh says, taking an uncertain step back. He looks at Jeremy and, when it becomes clear that Jeremy is going to say nothing more, he closes the door behind him.

Jeremy's father lets out a loud sigh and climbs down to the floor. He crosses his arms over the front of his flannel shirt and rocks back on his heels, eyes trained on the floor.

"So . . . that was awkward," he says.

Jeremy swallows hard. What's he supposed to do here? It's not like he can tell his father how he's really feeling. That in the last minute he felt like his heart was being ripped out of his chest over and over again. If Josh were named Jen, Jeremy might spill. But Josh is no Jen. And Jeremy's dad is not ready for a heart-to-heart about crushes on guys.

"Yeah," Jeremy says. It's all he's capable of saying.

"Jeremy, listen," his father says, rubbing the back of his neck. "About breakfast yesterday—"

"Dad, you don't have to—"

"No," his father says, stopping him cold with a stare that means business. "There's no way we're going to get through this if we don't talk about it."

Jeremy takes a deep breath. Leans back against the wall. "Okay."

"I didn't mean to say that *you* weren't normal," his father says, looking everywhere but at Jeremy. "I meant nothing *felt* normal. I've never had to welcome you home after weeks away. I've never not known what to say to you. And I'm betting you feel the same way."

Jeremy blinks as tears sting at his eyes, surprising him.

"Am I right?" his father asks.

"You're not wrong," Jeremy replies, putting his hands behind his back and pushing himself away from the wall, then letting himself fall back.

"Look . . . it may take a while," Jeremy's father says. "But we're going to get back there. I think the first thing we're going to have to do is admit that neither one of us is perfect."

Jeremy glances at his father. Up until about a month ago, he thought his father *was* perfect. And all he'd ever done was try to be the perfect son. But that wasn't the truth. And neither was the perfect vision he had of his father. They've both made mistakes, and they're going to make more.

But at least he knows that now.

Jeremy pushes himself away from the wall again and this time, he stands up straight. "Okay," he says with a nod. "Neither one of us is perfect."

His father presses his lips together. "I love you, kid," he says, the words blurring together.

Then he reaches over and pulls Jeremy into a tight, quick bear hug. In the two seconds Jeremy is pressed against his father, everything's okay. He knows that everything's going to be okay.

When Jeremy pulls away, he immediately hits the floor to clean up the mess he made and to avoid prolonging the mushiness for any longer. Right now it's as if just the right amount of emotion has been flushed out and if either of them lets anything else go, it's going to be overwhelming.

But as Jeremy starts to pile up the papers and folders into a nice, shredible stack, he realizes his hands are shaking. His heart still hasn't calmed down from seeing Josh. What was he thinking when he saw Jeremy? Does Josh want to talk to him as badly as Jeremy suddenly wants to talk to Josh?

What do I do now? Jeremy wonders. He has no idea what his next step with Josh should be, but he knows that he has to do something. Now that he's seen Josh again, inaction and avoidance are no longer options.

• • •

Peter can't feel anything but his heart. He can't see anything, hear anything, register anything, because his heart has taken over. It's pounding away quickly and violently, demanding his full attention.

"What is taking her so long?" Peter says under his

breath, clasping his hands together as he stares at a little clay statuette on Dr. Chang's desk.

"Try to relax, Peter," his mother tells him. But she doesn't look at him and doesn't move a muscle. Her own hands are clenched together so hard, little white spots have formed on her skin where her fingertips are pressing in. "Everything's going to be okay."

"I know," Peter says. It just hangs in the air, sounding none too convincing.

She's going to come in here and tell me that the swelling has gone down. It'll be just a matter of days before I can start trying to walk again, Peter tells himself, his eyes darting around the room. He looks at the clock, the door, the little blinking lights on the phone. A door slams somewhere out in the corridor and his heart attempts to leave his body via his throat.

Peter squeezes his eyes shut and reaches one hand into the pocket on the side of his wheelchair. He clasps the picture of himself and his six friends between his thumb and forefinger.

Think about something else, he urges himself. *Think about the prom. Yeah. Me and Meena,* walking *into the prom. She's wearing something simple and . . . light blue. All the guys are jealous when they see us—*

The door suddenly opens and in walks Dr. Chang. Peter's free hand grips the armrest on his chair. She looks at him quickly, then moves her gaze to his mother, giving them both her thin, noncommittal smile. It's impossible to read what she's thinking. She carries a folder that holds the key to Peter's life. She sinks into her leather chair, then pushes her hair away from her face.

The next few seconds seem to pass in excruciatingly slow motion. She places the folder on the desk. Opens it. Smooths it flat. Takes her glasses from the pocket of her white coat. Slips them on. Clears her throat. Folds her hands on top of the folder. Looks up. Smiles.

Say something, for God's sake! Say anything! Peter wails internally.

"It's not good news," she says.

Just don't say that.

Instinctively Peter looks at his mother. She smiles at him reassuringly, but her eyes are a strangled mess of worry, disappointment, fear. Her hands clench even harder.

"I'm sorry to tell you, Peter, that the swelling around your spinal cord has not gone down as significantly as we'd hoped," Dr. Chang says, looking him directly in the eye.

Peter starts to sweat. He hadn't thought it possible, but his heart has somehow found a way to pound harder. It wants out of his body and it wants out now. Peter feels exactly the same way.

"In fact, the swelling hasn't gone down at all," Chang continues. She looks down at the page in front of her, but it seems like an offhand gesture. She already knows what it says. It says no dice. You're screwed, buddy. Might as well start looking into those Special Olympics.

"What does that mean?" his mother manages to say. Her voice sounds as dry as Peter's throat feels.

"Basically, at this stage, in cases like these . . . the patient is usually confined to a wheelchair."

"Forever?" Peter hears himself say. It doesn't sound like him at all. It sounds like a whiny five-year-old cartoon character.

Chang's light blue eyes flick in his direction. They're full of sympathy. "Yes, I'm afraid so."

No. This isn't happening, Peter thinks wildly. *It was not supposed to be this way. What about the dreams and the . . . the warmth I've been feeling? What about all my friends? Helping them . . . being there for them . . . I thought there was a reason. This can't be it.*

"What about surgery?" Peter asks, pushing himself up straight in his chair. "I can have surgery, can't I?"

She shakes her head slowly, as if the motion is bringing her pain. "I'm sorry, Peter. It would be too risky. We could end up doing more harm than good. You could come out of it worse—"

"Worse?" Peter snaps, his face contorting with confused rage. "What could be worse?"

She takes a deep, patient breath. "You could lose the use of your arms as well."

A sob wells up in Peter's throat and he holds it back, making his eyes sting instantly with hot tears. He blinks and looks away, toward the window with its half-open blinds. A couple of young kids run by, one chasing the other, screaming and laughing. Somehow Peter feels like they're laughing at him.

It was all a lie. Everything I've been telling myself for weeks was a lie. It's not over. It will never be over. I'll never be forgiven for what I did. I'm just going to keep being punished and punished and punished. . . .

"So there's nothing . . . ?" Peter's mother says, her voice far, far away. "Nothing we can do?"

He feels like it's coming from somewhere above him and that he's falling farther away by the moment. He's tumbling down a long, dark hole and no one notices. No one cares. No one's ever going to be able to get him out.

"Barring a miracle, I'm afraid not," Dr. Chang says, the words floating somewhere far above Peter's mind. "You can come back in six weeks and we'll check again, but I wouldn't recommend pinning too many hopes on it."

She looks at Peter, but he barely realizes it. He's falling, spinning, tumbling. He's being enveloped by darkness.

"The best thing you can do for yourself now, Peter, is really start to adapt to your new way of life," she says.

Way of life . . . this is my way of life. . . .

There are good-byes. The doctor shakes his mother's hand. A door opens. Peter is vaguely aware of the fact that he's being moved. He hears a door click behind him. Blinks as the fluorescent light in the hallway assaults his eyes.

His mother is talking, but he can't make the words make sense. He can't see her. She's behind him. Pushing him. Talking in soothing tones. But she can't walk next to him. She can't look at him and reassure him and move at the same time. They'll never walk and talk together again. He'll never walk and talk with anybody ever again.

It's all your fault, a little voice in Peter's mind taunts him. *How could you have thought you'd be forgiven . . . redeemed? You can't be redeemed for what you did. You can't have a normal life. You can't have friends. You can't be loved.*

Suddenly Peter feels a stinging sensation in his hand. Something's cutting into his palm in a million places. He pulls up his arm and unclenches a fist that's so tight, his knuckles hurt from the strain. There, in his palm, is the picture of him and Karyn and Meena and Reed and Jeremy and Danny and Jane—crumbled into a jagged, sweaty, ball.

You can't have friends, the voice says again. *You can't be loved.*

CHAPTER FOUR

This can't be *good,* Meena thinks, looking up from her barely touched homework long enough to watch the clock on her desk change from 7:43 to 7:44 on Monday evening.

Peter should have called her by now. He has to be home from the doctor. If the news was good, he would have called her, right? So that means it must be bad. It must be very, very bad.

Meena swallows hard and glances at the phone on the other side of her desk.

"Okay, stop it," Meena tells herself. "You don't even know what's going on. Maybe he's out right now celebrating with his parents."

But telling herself that doesn't make the nervous dread pressing in on her go away. She knows from experience that there's not much in this world that will make that go away. Sleep, maybe. Or distraction. And at the moment her *American Nation* textbook is just not doing it for her.

If it's not Peter she's thinking of, it's Steven Clayton.

And when she starts to think of Steven and the police and the statement she's going to have to make, she tries to force herself to think of something else and then starts naturally thinking of Peter.

Meena pushes her chair away from her desk, grabs the cordless phone, and stands up. She has some phone calls to make. Some good, happy phone calls. If this doesn't take her mind off all the uncertainty, nothing will.

She leans down and pulls out the bottom drawer of her desk, using her free hand to sift through the papers and notebooks. Finally she spots the bright blue Falls High directory and yanks it out. Plopping down on her bed, Meena opens the little phone book to the *C* section and locates Danny Chaiken's number.

Ever since she had the idea to do this for Peter in homeroom today, she's been trying to think of who to call for help. And as strange as it is, the names that have come into her head are those of the very people who were there for *that* party. Peter's mentioned how he's been working out with Reed and Jeremy and how he's even had a couple of visits from Karyn. And of course, he and Jane have spent a lot of time talking since she's been helping him around school. But Peter seems particularly psyched about hanging around Danny again, so Meena figures he's a good place to start.

"Calling Danny Chaiken," Meena says under her breath as she dials. "There's something I never thought I'd do."

Placing the directory aside, she crosses her legs at the

knee and hugs her free arm over her stomach. Then she brings the phone to her ear and clicks her teeth together. The line barely has the chance to ring before Danny picks up.

"Chaiken's Bakery! Real butter makes the difference!"

Meena's brows scrunch together.

"Hello?" the voice says.

"Danny?" Meena asks.

"Yeah?"

"Oh, it's Meena Miller," Meena says. "I thought you said—"

"Oh . . . hey," Danny says, clearly surprised. "Sorry about the greeting. I just think it's funny."

"Oh . . . okay," Meena says.

"I guess it's not," Danny says flatly. "So what's up?"

It takes Meena a moment to recall what, exactly, she's doing on the phone. It's been long enough since she's called anyone from school, let alone someone she's not exactly friends with, and his greeting has thrown her.

"I . . . uh . . . Peter Davis's birthday is this Friday and I want to throw a party for him," Meena says. There's a pause that makes her feel the need to elaborate. "I know it's short notice, but I—"

"No! It's fine. I'm in," Danny says. "I'm totally, totally in. Just tell me when and where."

Meena smiles at his exuberance. Maybe this will be easier than she thought. But then, there's the one little detail that she knows is going to be extremely hard to tell him about—to tell all of them about. She decides it will be best to just get it out there.

"Well, it's gonna be Friday night and I spoke to his dad today and he seems to think that it would be best if we had it at their house, you know, because it's equipped for the wheelchair and everything. I guess they have a lift or something that goes down into the—um, downstairs. And I guess he just feels better having it where he can, you know, chaperon."

This silence is different. Weighted. Meena knew it was coming and she can feel it in her heart. Add that to the fact that she's just strung more words together than she had in weeks and she's starting to wish she never picked up the phone.

"You want to have it at the Davises' house?" Danny asks, surprised.

"I know," Meena says, biting her lip. "I was going to have it here, but my parents . . . it just isn't a great time for them. Mr. Davis seemed to think it would be okay."

She looks down at her lap and waits for Danny to back out. Not that she would blame him. It's going to be more than a little intense, being at that house. All of them. After all this time.

Meena tries to keep her mind from flipping over to the images of that day, but it doesn't work. The flashing lights. The blood. The shiny shoes of the police officer hovering over her and Jane and Karyn. It all fills her head until she manages to concentrate hard enough to push it back out.

Yes, it's going to be hard. But if Peter's father wants it at their house, that's where it's going to be. And Meena doesn't care if the rest of them say no. She's going to have this party if she's the only guest there.

"Yeah, we have a million steps here," Danny says. "So I guess Mr. Davis is right. What can I do to help?"

Meena pushes herself up and grabs her notebook off her desk. "Actually, if you could invite a few people for me, that would be cool."

There's no way she wants to try to have this conversation over and over again.

"Aye-aye, Captain," Danny says. "Who do you want me to call?"

Meena flips to the back of her notebook, where she'd written up a guest list earlier that afternoon. "Okay, we've got Keith, Max, Doug, Jane, Karyn, Reed, Jeremy—"

"Hold up," Danny says. "Reed Frasier and Jeremy Mandile? Do those two hang out with Peter?"

"Yeah. Peter's been working out with them lately," Meena says. "I'm sure he'd want them there."

"Interesting," Danny says. "Okay. I've got Keith and Max and those guys. And I'll call Jane and Jeremy. I'm sure one of them can call Reed and Karyn."

"Great," Meena says with a relieved sigh. "That just leaves me a few more. Thanks, Danny. And invite whoever else you want to have there, as long as the total doesn't go over twenty. Mr. Davis said we should keep it around there."

"Cool," Danny says. "I'll talk to you later."

After Meena hangs up the phone, she puts a check next to Danny's name. As she flips through the directory again, she realizes she's found the perfect thing to distract her. It's been too long since she felt such a sense of purpose, and it's all for a good cause.

Peter deserves to have someone do something nice for him. And it will be good for him to be surrounded by friends and to have some fun. If he *did* get bad news today, maybe it will help take his mind off things a bit.

Meena glances at the silent phone again and sighs. Now if he would just call her . . .

• • •

"It'll cause total mayhem," Keith Kleiner says. "Think about it."

"Yeah, I'm sure it will, man," Danny says into the phone. After debating the pros and cons of stink bombs with Keith for the last fifteen minutes, he still hasn't managed to get a straight answer out of him about Peter's party. "So are you in, or are you out?"

"What? Oh! I'll try to make it," Keith says.

Danny rolls his eyes. Same answer he'd gotten from Max Kang and Doug Anderson. Like these guys have so many more worthy plans. What are they going to do instead? Go up to the Falls and throw beer bottles at rocks?

"Cool. Well, I'll see you tomorrow," Danny says.

He hangs up the phone before Keith can even say

good-bye, mostly because the kid probably wanted to keep talking about his odiferous ideas for a senior prank.

"Stink bombs," Danny says under his breath. "Amateur."

He flips through his Falls High directory until he finds Jeremy Mandile's number and quickly dials. He wants to get this task over with fast so he can call Cori before trying to do his homework. So far, it's been a fairly lucid day, but he's never sure when the brain fog might roll in and he wants to get as much done as he can before it does.

Working around it, Danny says to himself as the phone starts to ring. *Staying positive. I'm not annoyed that the meds run my life. Not at all.*

"Hello?"

"Jeremy? It's Danny," he says, feeling a little strange since they're not exactly phone buddies.

"Danny? Hey, man," Jeremy says. "What's up?"

"It's party time, my friend," Danny says, leaning back against his bed. "This Friday night Meena's throwing a birthday party for Peter Davis. At his house."

Just saying it makes his stomach clench painfully, however nonchalant he tries to sound. Clearly it has the same effect on Jeremy because all Danny can hear is the guy breathing on the other end of the line.

"Ya there?" Danny asks, trying to make like it's no big deal.

"Yeah, I'm here," Jeremy says, a bit strained. "And I'll, uh, I mean I guess I'll . . ." Another long pause. "I'll

63

be there," he finally says, still sounding a bit uncertain.

"Good," Danny says. Jeremy's a stand-up guy, the type that can get past the past. He's been cool with Danny ever since the car accident where Danny put his little sister, Emily, in danger. "Okay, I already called Jane and she said she'd call Reed. What about Karyn?"

"Don't worry. I'm sure Reed will tell her," Jeremy says, his voice slowly normalizing with each word. "Hey, I'll bring the music."

Danny snorts a laugh and his eyes dart to his massive CD collection. "Dude, I don't think so. I'm on music."

"No way, man!" Jeremy retorts. "Like everyone really wants to listen to house music all night."

"Please! The fact that you just said that proves how very much *I* need to be the DJ," Danny says. "At least I won't be spinning Aerosmith all night."

"What's wrong with Aerosmith?" Jeremy asks.

"Nothing. If you're forty," Danny replies, sitting up and pulling his legs in to sit Indian style. "And don't even start with me about the whole 'Armageddon' song and how huge it was. That song sucks."

Jeremy laughs. "All right, all right. I'll just bring some CDs—how's that?"

"Fine. We'll use 'em as coasters," Danny jokes.

"Whatever, man. I'll see you tomorrow," Jeremy says.

Danny hangs up the phone and it rings instantly, causing his heart to jump. He clicks it on.

"Hello?"

"Isn't reality TV over yet?" Cori's voice demands. "I mean, come on! Now we have to have crossovers? Who wants to see the cast of *Survivor* eating sheep eyes on *Fear Factor*?"

"I do!" Danny says, reaching for his remote.

"You need help," Cori replies. "So, what's going on?"

"Party," Danny says, clicking on his TV. "Peter Davis's house. Friday night. Birthday thing. You there?"

"Absolutely," Cori says. "Anything I can bring? Chips . . . dip . . . pudding-wrestling paraphernalia."

Danny drops his remote. "You *have* pudding-wrestling paraphernalia?"

"No," Cori says.

"Damn," Danny jokes. "But seriously. You don't have to bring anything but your beautiful self."

Argh! Did I really just say that?

"Okay," Cori says. "Let's pretend you didn't just channel the spirit of Don Johnson. Seriously, Danny, I want to help. Give me a task."

Danny grins and picks at the little fuzzies on the flannel throw at the foot of his bed. "Well, I could use your spinning equipment," he says, flicking a fuzz ball into the air. "I've given myself the job of DJ."

"God help us all," Cori says with a laugh. Then she sighs resignedly. "Okay. My motherboard is your motherboard."

"A woman after my own heart," Danny says.

• • •

"Hello?"

"Hey . . . Reed? It's Jane Scott," Jane says into the phone as she paces around her bedroom.

She's been pacing in circles ever since Danny called her a little while ago and she's making herself a bit dizzy. But at this point, she's afraid if she stops, she'll have a head-spinning problem of Tilt-A-Whirl proportions, so she just keeps going.

"You don't have to say your last name, Jane. I know who you are," Reed says with a good-natured laugh.

Blushing furiously, Jane grips the phone a little tighter. "Oh, okay. Yeah. Of course," she fumbles out. *Just talk, stupid.* "Listen, I'm calling to invite you to this birthday party Meena Miller is throwing for Peter on Friday night."

"Oh yeah?" Reed says, intrigued. "I thought you didn't do parties."

Jane laughs. "I know, can you believe it? Two parties in two weeks. Whip out the record books."

"So where and what time?" Reed asks.

"It's gonna be at Peter's house at eight," Jane says a bit too brightly.

"Oh. Really?" Reed says just as brightly. "That's—"

"Yeah. I know," Jane says, cutting him off so he doesn't have to say something neither of them wants to hear. The last thing she wants to do is have a conversation about the very thing she's been trying to avoid thinking about ever since Danny called her.

"Are they gonna have it in the—"

"Yeah, I guess so," Jane answers. "The basement's the only room big enough for a party. And I guess they have one of those lift things, to bring Peter down there."

The basement. What are they thinking? Why would his parents want to have another birthday party in that basement? Jane's mind races with questions. *Why didn't they move out of that house years ago? How can they even* live *there, let alone throw a party. . . .*

"Oh." He clears his throat. "Okay. Right."

Jane takes a deep breath. She'd hoped Reed would think this was no big deal. He's the jock. The number-one man on campus. The guy with the plan, with the answers. Nothing is supposed to faze him. And the fact that he's obviously thrown by this makes her throat suddenly feel so tight, she can barely breathe.

All those memories. All those images. The blood seeping into the rug. Did they get the stain out? Could they possibly have gotten the stain out?

Jane shudders. *Focus. Just focus. This is a happy occasion. Yeah, right.*

"So, listen, I was thinking it would be cool if we brought a couple of cakes or pies from work," Jane says. "What do you think?"

"Sounds good. I can pick them up before I head over there on Friday," Reed says.

"Good," Jane replies, still walking. "Get chocolate. For some reason I remember that Peter likes chocolate."

"Not a problem," Reed replies. "So . . . when are you working this week?"

Jane finally stops and her brain takes a second to catch up. She lowers herself carefully onto her bed and squeezes her eyes shut to stop the world from spinning.

"Uh . . . at the moment, I can't remember," she says, bringing a hand to her face.

"You okay?" Reed asks, his voice concerned.

"Yeah," Jane replies. "Hey! You know what's weird? I don't think I've ever actually called you before." A few weeks ago she would have been afraid to call Reed just because she would be worried that *he'd* think Jane Scott calling him was weird. Huh. She's come a long way.

Reed chuckles. "Hey. Call me anytime," he says, causing Jane to smile. "So, anything else I can do besides pick up the dessert?"

"Actually, if you could call Karyn and tell her about the party, that would be great," she says. There's a long silence and Jane narrows her eyes. "Reed? I can do it if you don't—"

"No! I've got it. I'll call her," Reed says quickly.

"Okay," Jane says. "So, I'll see you in history tomorrow."

"Yep. I'll be there," Reed says.

Jane hangs up the phone and reaches down to the floor next to her bed for her big, fat SAT prep book, actually looking forward to the distraction.

• • •

"Okay, you can do this," Reed tells himself, staring down at his cell phone like it's about to blow.

He's standing on the porch behind his house with the outside light on, watching his breath make clouds in the frigid air. Somehow he couldn't bring himself to make this phone call inside the house. His mother, who is already not exactly speaking to him, might overhear something that could give her a coronary.

First Reed takes her precious T. J.'s spot on the team, and now he's taking T. J.'s girl? She'd lose it.

Not that he and Karyn will probably be saying anything suspicious. Karyn made it pretty clear in the cafeteria today that she's in no hurry to talk about what, exactly, their kiss meant.

Shaking ever so slightly—from the cold of course—he hits the speed dial button for Karyn's number, closes his eyes, and brings the phone to his ear. *It's just Karyn. Don't be a moron.*

"Hello?" she says breathlessly, as if she's just run up the stairs to grab the phone.

"Hey."

There's a pause. "Hey."

It's distant. Hesitant. Like she's wondering why the hell she just ran up the stairs to get *this* call.

"Hey," he says again.

"Hey."

"Okay, now that we've established that . . . ," Reed says with a small laugh.

Karyn laughs as well. "Yeah . . . we know lots of words," she says.

He imagines her sitting down on her bed. Pulling a throw pillow onto her lap and hugging it to her. Or maybe twirling her long blond hair around one finger.

But why does she sound so tense? Does she not want to talk to him? When was the last time she didn't want to talk to him?

Two weeks ago, a little voice in his mind answers. For best friends, their relationship hasn't been without complications lately.

"Reed?" Karyn says. "Are you still there?"

"Yeah. Sorry. I'm just calling to invite you to a party on Friday night," Reed says, rubbing his freezing, yet somehow sweat-soaked palm on his jeans. He looks in the window and sees that his face is bright red. Is it from the cold or the nervousness? "Meena is having a birthday party for Peter at his house."

"Wow," Karyn says.

"Yeah," Reed replies.

"Well . . . I'll be there . . . I guess," she says uncertainly. In his mind's eye she's now definitely clutching the pillow. "I'll be there," she adds more firmly.

"Cool," Reed says.

"That's kind of weird, huh? Meena throwing a party for Peter, I mean," Karyn says. "She's been pretty out of it lately. I haven't even talked to her in, I don't know, a *while*."

"Yeah, me neither," Reed says. "But she's been hanging with Peter a lot."

"Yeah. I guess so," Karyn says. "I wonder how she's doing."

"Well, you should talk to her," Reed says, glad for the moment to be on a topic other than him and Karyn.

"Maybe I will," Karyn says.

Then it happens. The inevitable awkward pause.

"So . . . ," Reed says.

"So . . . ," Karyn repeats.

Reed takes a deep breath. This is not a good sign. What is Karyn thinking? What is she actually going to say to him when they finally have their little talk?

What if she thinks Friday night was a mistake?

Maybe we shouldn't talk, Reed thinks. *Ever again.*

That way he'll be able to avoid hearing her reject him. Hearing her say, "Listen, Reed, you're a really nice guy, but—"

It's not like he's never heard it before. He just doesn't think he can take hearing it from Karyn.

But he also can't take this silence.

"So when do you want to talk?" he asks her, hoping against hope that she won't say right now. His heart has had about as much as it can handle for one night.

"Tomorrow," Karyn replies. "Definitely tomorrow. After school."

"Good. Sounds good," he says. "I'll see you then."

Reed hangs up before the tension has a chance to envelop him. The thing is, Reed knows that Friday night was a mistake—on some level. Even though it had been the most incredible few hours of his life—kissing Karyn, talking with her, feeling comfortable with the fact that he likes her and she likes him.

But it was all just a fairy tale. Because in the real world, Reed's brother is still in love with Karyn. And in the real world, Reed isn't entirely sure that he has it in him to break his brother's heart—again.

The question is, does he have it in him to back away from Karyn when he finally has the chance to be with her—the chance he's been waiting for and dreaming of for years? He doesn't think so.

"This sucks," Reed says aloud, his voice slicing through the silent night air.

He looks down and spots his basketball, sitting in the corner of the porch with a few dead, dried leaves on it. Without a second thought, he grabs the ball and heads for the driveway to shoot some hoops. Nothing like a little exercise in the freezing cold to clear his mind.

● ● ●

It's ringing, Jeremy tells himself, using every ounce of strength in his soul to resist hanging up. *There's no turning back now. If you hang up, he's going to know it was you. A hang up on the exact day that you saw each other after more than a month of not seeing each other? Yeah. He'll know.*

Besides, he probably has caller ID. Whoever came up with that invention should be thrown in jail.

By the fourth ring, however, Jeremy's nerves are entirely frayed. His hand is on its way down toward the cradle with the receiver when someone finally picks up.

"Hello?"

Dammit!

He brings the phone back up to his ear. "Hi, Josh," he says. He sounds amazingly cool and collected, considering his heart is in his mouth.

"Jeremy," Josh replies. Not a question. He recognizes the voice. Was probably expecting this call.

"I guess you're not surprised I called," Jeremy says, lowering himself onto the chair in front of his desk.

"Well . . . kind of, I guess," Josh says. "I was definitely surprised to see you today."

"Yeah. Hey! How did your auditions go?" He rolls his eyes at himself the second the words are out of his mouth. After all this time, an attempt at a regular conversation is ridiculous.

"Good. Thanks for asking," Josh says. "So, you're back at work now."

"Yeah," Jeremy says. He crosses his fingers, then plunges on. "Listen, I'm sorry I didn't call sooner. It's just been . . ."

"Insane?" Josh says. "I figured."

"Insane barely covers it," Jeremy replies, relaxing a bit at Josh's casual tone. "But it's still not right. I never apologized for . . . everything."

73

"No need," Josh says. "Really, man. I understand."

"Still, I shouldn't have taken it out on you like that, and I'm sorry," Jeremy says, trying not to shudder as he recalls the way he flipped out on Josh for showing up at Falls High just when all the gay rumors were circulating. It seems like so long ago now, but he still remembers the intensity of his misplaced anger.

"Apology accepted," Josh says.

Jeremy lets out a sigh of relief and leans back against the chair, feeling suddenly exhausted. But he still has to do what he called to do. Danny had offered up a prime opportunity earlier tonight, and Jeremy isn't going to let it go by. That is, if he can keep from chickening out long enough to finish the whole sentence.

"So . . . there's this party one of my friends is throwing on Friday night . . . ," Jeremy begins.

If he cuts me off, I'll just let it go, he tells himself. *Don't get in too far.*

"Yeah?" Josh asks. He sounds interested. A little mini-Jeremy does a cartwheel inside his head.

"And I was wondering if you'd want to go," Jeremy says. He clears his throat. He's about to add the words "with me" but stops himself before it's too late, his pulse pounding as if he's just gotten himself caught in a trap. He doesn't want to imply that this is a date because he's not sure he's quite ready for a date . . . yet. But he doesn't want to say that it's not, either. He doesn't have a clue what he's doing now that he's in the thick of it.

Why did I call? Jeremy asks himself. *Do I really love pain or something?*

"That sounds cool," Josh says finally.

"Yeah?" Jeremy asks, his voice a couple of octaves higher than usual.

"Yeah," Josh replies. "But I think we should get together first and talk."

Jeremy blinks. Interesting. And mildly disconcerting. "Oh," he says. "Okay." Though he has no idea what he's agreeing to. What does Josh want to talk about?

"Why don't we meet up tomorrow night at the diner?" Josh asks. "Around seven?"

"Okay. I'll see you then," Jeremy says.

When he hangs up the phone, he feels like he should be relieved that he finally got it over with. He's been thinking about calling Josh for days and now he's done it. Mission accomplished. And with not bad results.

But something isn't quite right. There's still a lot of uncertainty clouding his thoughts. And now he knows he's going to be nervous all day in school tomorrow. All he can do is hope that soon enough, he'll be laughing at himself. Because maybe, just maybe, he'll have found out there was nothing to be nervous about.

CHAPTER FIVE

Tuesday morning, the door to Peter's room opens slowly, tentatively. Peter presses his face into his pillow and pulls his comforter up over the back of his head. He doesn't want light to touch him. He doesn't want to look at anyone, talk to anyone. He doesn't want to move.

It's not like I really can, anyway, so what's the point? he thinks as he waits for his mother to figure out what to say. He knows it's her standing in the doorway. He heard his father leave for an early shift at the police station hours ago.

"Peter . . . are you going to get up?" his mother asks finally.

Peter doesn't answer. He doesn't have it in him to formulate the word.

"Okay, honey, you can stay home today. I understand," she tells him. As if it matters what she says. He wouldn't get out of this bed if she told him the house was on fire.

The door swings shut again.

It's all my fault. It was all a lie. It's all my fault. It was all a lie.

The same two sentences have been repeating in his brain over and over again since the moment he hit his bed late yesterday afternoon. And the longer he thinks about it, the more clear the truth becomes.

Everything he's believed for the past few weeks has been bull. He wasn't brought back together with his old friends to help them. He didn't become part of their lives again as some kind of redemption. That warm feeling he was experiencing was a hallucination. Or worse—a cosmic joke. All these things conspired to make him think he was being forgiven. That he was being redeemed. But in truth he was just being set up for the big fall. The big punishment.

Right now there is some otherworldly force out there having a good laugh at Peter's expense.

"You thought you were being forgiven for what you've done! But you'll never *be forgiven! You're not worth it!"*

"He wouldn't have come if I hadn't pushed so hard," Peter mumbles into his sheets. He shivers and pulls his comforter more tightly around his shoulders, but it makes no difference.

Where is the warmth now? Where is his comfort?

You don't deserve any comfort, a little voice in his head taunts him.

Harris would never have come to that party if he hadn't been such a nice kid. If he hadn't wanted Peter to be his best friend so badly. He was sick. He had a bad cold. But did he listen to his mother and stay in bed? No. He begged until she brought him over to Peter's house. And why?

"Because I wanted that stupid plane," Peter mutters, his heart thumping painfully. "If I hadn't talked nonstop about that thing, he wouldn't have even *been* here."

But that's not even the worst of Peter's blame and he knows it. His hands grasp at the sheet beneath him as he tries to fight away the memories that threaten to absorb him. But he doesn't have the energy to fight them off anymore.

And he deserves to remember it. He deserves to have it haunt him.

All that blood. The screaming. The flashing lights. His mother crying and clutching his father. Mrs. Driver's slack-jawed expression when she saw her son. The crisp white sheet. The stains. The little red splatters all over Karyn's tear-drenched face.

And hanging over the whole scene—red, blue, and green streamers, a glittering Happy Birthday sign, balloons and plates and hats and cups and favors that Peter had picked out himself the day before. All that projected happiness. All that very real misery.

Unbidden, a group of childlike voices start to sing the birthday song in Peter's mind.

"Happy birthday to you . . . Happy birthday to you . . ."

"Peter? Do you need anything?"

Peter's heart drops from the surprise of the sudden interruption. His mother is still standing there? He hadn't realized. Or maybe she'd left and come back. He has no sense of time. No sense of anything but his desperate hopelessness.

"Well . . . let me know if you do," she says, sounding incredibly tired. "I'll call the school and let them know you won't be in."

Who cares if you call the school? he thinks. *I'm never going back there. I'm never going anywhere. Never again.*

• • •

"So . . . how was practice today?" Karyn asks as Reed drives his Subaru Outback down the street on Tuesday after school. She tries to look interested. Eyes wide. Watching him. She's an awful actress and she knows it. No one in this car thinks they're here to talk about football.

"Fine," Reed says, eyes trained on the road. "How was yours?"

"Fine," Karyn answers. "You think you're ready for the semifinals?"

He sighs. "Yeah. We'll be ready."

He glances at her out of the corner of his eye and Karyn feels her body temperature go up about a thousand degrees. She knows he's waiting for her to say something. And he knows that she knows he's waiting for her to say something. But what?

Well, Reed, sorry to mess with your head, but I can't go out with you.

"So, where do you want to go? Friendly's . . . Phil's . . . the diner . . . ?" he asks.

79

Suddenly the idea of sitting down at a restaurant with him—of trying to eat while having the conversation they need to have—makes even Karyn's fingernails tense up. She has to get it over with now. Then he'll either boot her out of the car, or they'll get past it and have a semi-uncomfortable meal. But whatever the consequences, it will have to be better than this dread.

"Reed, here's the thing," she says, eliciting another sidelong glance. He pales slightly, picking up on the negative intro. Karyn takes a deep breath and squeezes her eyes shut. "I just don't think I can have a boyfriend right now."

Suddenly the car jerks to the right and Reed guns it into the wide-open parking lot of Reagan Elementary—stopping right next to the jungle gym where they first met. A nice coincidence. He puts the car in park and turns to look at her. A pained look creases his features momentarily and he looks away again, out the windshield toward the tiny-looking front door of the school. Karyn's heart pounds away at the silence as she waits for him to speak.

But then she can't wait anymore.

"Reed—"

"You can't have a boyfriend right now or you can't have me as a boyfriend?" he asks flatly.

"No. That's not it at all," Karyn says, leaning forward in an attempt to attract his attention away from whatever he's staring at. It doesn't work, so she just keeps talking. "Reed, that kiss—I mean, the first one, at my house—it changed everything for me. After that, I knew you weren't just my best friend. I knew there was more between us. A lot more. And even with how confusing things have been in the past couple of weeks, I still know that's true."

He turns his head slightly in her direction, but doesn't meet her gaze.

"It's why I broke up with T. J.," she continues. Then she stops, shaking her head. "No, see, that's the problem, right there. I didn't just break up with T. J. because I realized I had feelings for you. I broke up with T. J. because I realized that I'm *not* in love with *him*. But my feelings for you, they were all mixed in there. It should have just been about me, but it wasn't. It was about me and him, me and you. . . ." She trails off, then takes a deep breath. "I know this is going to sound insane but . . . I just . . . I've *always* had a boyfriend. I usually don't even have two days between them. Before T. J. it was Ray and before him it was Sean and before him it was Chris and before him it was Peter—"

"Trust me, I know your romantic history, okay?" Reed says, his voice filled with hurt. "And you forgot about Tristan."

Karyn's blush deepens and her heart turns over in her chest. How long has it been for him? How long has he been watching her and waiting and being the best friend she's ever had all the while? She looks down at her hands and gathers her thoughts before she starts speaking again.

"Reed, the last thing I want to do is hurt you . . . but I don't want to be one of those girls who can't exist without a boyfriend, you know?" she says, hoping she's making some sort of sense. "I don't want to jump from T. J. to you, without having a chance to be sure of everything I feel, everything I want. I need to be by myself for a while. I don't—I don't want to be my mother."

Reed finally looks at her, but his eyes are unreadable. Is it pity? Confusion? Disbelief?

"You're not your mother," he says firmly.

Karyn's eyes well up with tears. "Not yet, anyway," she says.

Reed's hand moves from the steering wheel, just a few inches, but then he seems to think better of whatever he was going to do and grasps the wheel again. Karyn suddenly wants to just crawl over there and curl up in his arms and let him tell her everything's going to be okay.

But she can't. That's the point. She can't always let some guy say a few words and pretend everything is okay. She has to be okay on her own.

Finally Reed lets out a loud sigh. "I understand . . . I guess," he says. He hooks his fingertips through the bottom of the steering wheel. "I mean . . . I do understand. To be honest, I was thinking it's probably a little soon . . . you know . . . with T. J."

Karyn's heart twists all over again. How did she get into this between-brothers mess in the first place?

"Not that I was going to do anything about it," Reed says with a chuckle.

Karyn's lips pull up at the ends. For once she's the

stronger one. She was able to tell Reed no, while he knew he'd never be able to do the same.

"How is T. J. doing?" she asks, turning so that her shoulder is against the back of her seat. "With the scholarship thing, I mean."

"Not so good, I don't think," Reed replies. He lifts his baseball cap from his head and scratches at his red hair, then pulls the cap back on tightly. "It's hard to tell since he still won't talk to me."

Karyn takes a deep breath and turns to gaze out the windshield at the playground—the chipped red paint on the monkey bars, one of the swings with its chains looped over and over and over again until the seat is hanging just inches from the bar. It looks really, really lonely.

"So maybe it's for the best, then, if we just give it a little while . . . ," she says slowly.

"Is that what we're doing?" Reed says, unable to hide the hopeful tone. "Just . . . giving it a little while?"

Karyn nods. "I think so. Yeah. If that's okay with you," she says.

"Yeah," Reed replies. "I think I can handle that."

She turns her head to look at him again and he's smiling. Karyn can't believe the effect that smile has on her now. All she wants to do is lace her hands through his and tell him to drive them off into the night.

"So . . . friends?" she says, using every ounce of her will

to resist the urge to hug him, to kiss him, to go the easy route and take it all back. "For now?"

"Friends," Reed repeats. "For now."

And then *he* hugs *her*. And when he stops, it's all Karyn can do to let him go.

• • •

Jeremy stops outside the glass double doors to the diner and takes a quick survey of the inside, hoping Josh isn't sitting at the very first booth, watching him hesitate. He finally spots the back of Josh's head. He's sitting at a table near the corner, facing the back wall.

Jeremy's already out of control nerves go even more haywire at the sight of him. He runs his hand over his short brown hair, still wet from the postpractice shower, and clenches both hands into fists, steeling himself.

"Just chill, man," he tells himself under his breath. "You'll be fine."

He grasps the cold door handle, pulls it open confidently, and strides into the restaurant.

Moments later, he slides onto the vinyl bench across from Josh. "Hey," he says. "How's it going?"

"It's good," Josh says, with a little nod. "It's going good."

"Good." Jeremy has absolutely no idea what to say next. He grabs a crusty, faux-leather-covered menu from the little holder against the wall and flips it open, though his whacked-out stomach has no intention of eating. Or at least no intention of *digesting*.

"Look, Jeremy, the reason I wanted to get together was to ask you about this party," Josh says, leaning his forearms on the table.

Good. Right to the point, Jeremy thinks, even as his heart pounds nervously. "What about it?" he asks, going for carefree.

"Are we going to this party as friends or as . . . more than friends?" Josh asks, raising his eyebrows. "I mean, I know we haven't talked in a while, so I'm not totally sure what you're thinking. . . ."

A nervous laugh somehow escapes from Jeremy's otherwise frozen body. "That's the question, I guess," he says. He looks down at the menu, fiddling with the fraying corner. "I guess I was hoping we could go as . . ."

He has one second to keep himself from saying it. But he can't.

"More than friends," he finishes, risking a glance up at Josh.

Josh smiles a kind smile and shifts in his seat, his eyes darting away for a millisecond. Suddenly Jeremy knows he's going to be let down easy. All the nervousness rushes out of him and is replaced by a much heavier feeling of disappointment.

Good job, Mandile. Your first try at a life and you crash and burn.

"Jeremy, I *really* like you. A lot," Josh says sincerely. "And that's why I think we should just be friends."

Jeremy blinks, not entirely sure that what he just heard

makes any sense. "Okay," he says uncertainly, flipping the menu cover open and closed, open and closed.

"I know, it sounds weird, but you've been through a lot lately," Josh says, lowering his voice. "You came out, you broke up with your girlfriend, you had to deal with everything at school, you fought with your parents—your mom even told me you moved out for a while. . . ."

Jeremy squirms a bit, concentrating on the menu now with every fiber of his being. Nothing like having every sordid detail of your life laid out by a potential boyfriend to make you want to run for the hills.

"I know how hard all that is," Josh continues. "And to be honest, I can't imagine that you'd be ready for . . . you know . . . a relationship right now."

Taking a deep breath and letting it out slowly, Jeremy looks into Josh's brown eyes and tries not to sound too hurt. "So, basically, you don't want to go out with someone who's such a mess."

"That's not it," Josh says. Then he smiles and adds, "Well, that's part of it. But I'm thinking of you, too. Come on, do you really want to throw your first guy-guy relationship into the mix right now?"

"Well, when you put it that way . . . ," Jeremy says with a small laugh. If he's going to be with Josh, he'd like it to work. And in order for it to work, he probably shouldn't come into it with everything else he has to deal with weighing him down.

But that doesn't change the fact that he's dying to kiss Josh again. Dying to find out what it would be like to be with him. It doesn't change the fact that right now everything hurts.

"I guess you're right," Jeremy says finally. Reluctantly.

"I'm not saying I don't want to hang out with you, because I do," Josh says. "I still want to go to this party."

Jeremy smiles and finally lets go of the menu. He can't help but feel let down. More like thrown down. Dropped. Stepped on. But at least Josh isn't saying good-bye for good.

"Hey, kids. Can I take your order?"

Jeremy's stomach suddenly growls. He looks up to find Norma, the ever-present gum-snapping waitress, hovering above their table. She has a big, hot pink lipstick mark on her cheek as if someone just gave her a wet kiss hello. Jeremy tries not to laugh and tears his eyes away.

"Cheeseburger, fries, and a Coke, please," Jeremy says.

"I'll have a chef's salad and some more water, please," Josh says. "And . . . uh . . . you've got some lipstick on your face there."

Josh hands her his napkin and a pleasant, warm feeling rushes over Jeremy. Josh is such a good guy. Jeremy was just going to let her walk around like that because he was too embarrassed to say anything. Why did Josh have to go and do something that nice just seconds after telling him they aren't going to be together?

"Thanks, sweetie," Norma says, laughing her truck-driver

laugh as she wipes it away. She scribbles into her pad, then puts her hands on her hips and looks from Jeremy to Josh and back again. "Now, who do I give the check to when you're done? 'Cuz usually I like to give it to the boyfriend, but it looks like I got two of 'em at this table."

Jeremy's face burns and he glances at Josh, whose expression mirrors his own. How can she tell? Forget figuring out that they're both gay, but did she really pick up on the attraction here?

If it's that noticeable, maybe there is *some hope,* Jeremy thinks. Who knows what the future will bring?

"I'll just let ya fight over it," Norma says with a wink before strolling off.

The moment she's gone, Jeremy and Josh burst out laughing.

• • •

Meena stands on the porch at Peter's house on Tuesday evening, shivering against a cold wind. She glances back at her car, sitting in the driveway, and considers getting right back behind the wheel and taking off before anyone can spot her. This isn't easy, this confronting potentially awful situations. She's avoided all confrontation for so long, she's not sure she's going to be any good at it.

But Peter may need her. He wasn't in school. He hasn't called her. The more time passes, the harder it is to believe that nothing bad happened at his doctor's appointment. And Meena is not going to just avoid him and wait for him to get in touch with her. She owes him this much.

And there's a tiny little selfish reason for her visit as well. It's going to happen tomorrow. The meeting with the police. Her parents told her when she came home today, and she can think of little else. Peter and the police. Peter and the police. She's gotten so used to telling Peter everything—to letting him comfort her—she's hoping against hope that he's fine, that they can talk. That they can be there for each other.

She reaches out one gloved finger and rings the doorbell. Her stomach is in knots as she waits. *Maybe they're not home. Maybe I should just go . . .*

"Hello, Meena!" Peter's mother says in a loud, chipper voice as she swings open the door. "Come in! Come in!"

Meena's heart thumps hard, but she smiles and slips into the warm house. This is a good sign. Peter's mother wouldn't be so cheerful if Peter had found out he was never going to walk again, right? But when Mrs. Davis turns to her again, there's an unmistakable sorrow behind her eyes that makes Meena's blood run cold. Maybe not.

"Peter will be so glad to see you!" she says, pressing her hands together. "Just let me go tell him you're here."

Mrs. Davis disappears through a door to Meena's right and Meena stands in the middle of the entryway, coat on, wool hat pulled down over her forehead, feeling completely awkward and conspicuous.

Please just let him be okay, she thinks. *Just let him be okay.*

Suddenly Meena hears raised voices coming from the

direction of Peter's room. They're muffled, but they're definitely raised. Peter and his mother are arguing.

Meena takes an instinctive step toward the door. Peter obviously doesn't want to see her. She should just go. Get out. Run as far as possible. Then she hears a door open and she freezes. Moments later, Peter's mother returns, followed by Peter. His face is all creased on one side and his eyes sag. He's wearing a flannel shirt over pajama pants. Just looking at him is enough to make Meena want to cry.

"Hey," she says uncertainly.

There isn't a trace of the light he normally has in his eyes when he sees her. Meena hadn't even realized it was there until now. Now that it's gone.

"Hey," he replies. Then he slowly looks up at his mother.

"I'll just leave you two alone," Mrs. Davis says before scurrying back to the kitchen. She shoots Meena a hopeful look over her shoulder and it makes Meena feel suddenly panicked. She can't do anything. She can't help anyone. She's not up to it. Why did she ever come here?

You came for Peter, a little voice in her mind reminds her firmly. *Look at him. He needs you.*

Peter makes no move to go into the living room or back to his room, so Meena simply stands there. Her hands are starting to itch, so she pulls her gloves off.

"So, you weren't in school today . . . ," Meena says.

"Yeah, I'm sick," Peter replies, looking off to the right.

Meena glances over to see what he's looking at but sees

nothing other than an overstuffed coatrack. She wants to ask him about the doctor's appointment so badly, but she can't seem to make the words come to her mouth.

If Peter wanted to talk about it, he would, she tells herself. *Just let him—*

"The doctors don't know anything, if you're wondering," Peter blurts suddenly. When he looks up at her, it's as if his green eyes are on fire. Like he's angry. "The tests were inconclusive, so . . . we just have to wait some more."

"Oh," Meena says. Is that bad or good? Bad, most likely, since it means he's not better. But there's still a chance he *could* get better, so . . .

So why doesn't she believe him? When she really looks at him, he can't hold her gaze. He keeps looking at his hands, the floor, the coatrack. Peter is never this evasive.

And he's not sick. He's depressed, Meena realizes. She knows the difference. She's used the sick line enough herself.

But if he's not going to tell her what's going on, she can't make him. If there's one thing Meena knows from firsthand experience, it's that pressing someone for information is the best way to make them clam up.

"Wanna go watch TV?" Meena asks.

"Actually, I'm kind of tired," Peter says tonelessly.

Meena's stomach turns, but she tries not to let her disappointment, her fear, her sorrow, show.

"Peter are . . . are you okay?" Meena asks finally, even though she knows he's not. It's fairly obvious he's not.

"Yeah. Just tired," he repeats. He's already turning to go.

Don't just leave, Meena thinks. *Talk to me!* But it's clear that the last thing Peter wants to do right now is talk.

"Okay, well, hopefully I'll see you in school tomorrow, then," she says.

"Yeah." It's more a sarcastic exhalation than a word. He turns the wheels on his chair again and starts out the door. "See ya."

Before Meena's heart even has the chance to finish breaking for him, she hears his door slam with a chilling finality.

CHAPTER SIX

They're talking about *me,* Peter thinks, slumping down in his chair and staring at the bottom edge of the Yankee poster on his bedroom wall on Wednesday morning. His father put it there when he moved into this wheelchair-accessible room from his old one. Peter doesn't even follow baseball.

They don't know me, but they're talking about me. They're wondering what they're going to do with me now.

His parents both stayed home from work today. They're in the kitchen right now, talking in low tones, but even from two rooms away, Peter can tell they're stressed.

And why shouldn't they be? They have a cripple for a son. A permanent cripple.

Peter takes a deep breath and moves his eyes to his closed blinds. Where did he go wrong? How did he end up in this place? This place where everything is gray and black and formless and pointless and wrong.

Was it the hoping? If he'd never bothered to hope, would he have been able to fall this far?

A vision of Meena floats through his mind. Meena and her concerned expression, standing in the entryway the day before, looking like she wanted to run for dear life. Looking at him like she feels sorry for him.

Peter slides even lower in the seat, his heart dragging him down. He had so many plans for him and Meena. He was going to be her boyfriend. He was going to take her to the prom. He was going to dance with her.

What a laugh.

"I'm so pathetic," Peter says through his teeth. He lifts his fist and brings it down, hard, on his right thigh.

But he feels nothing.

"Pathetic, loser, freak, moron . . ."

He punches himself over and over again, tears of frustration stinging his eyes. Meena never wanted him. Would never want him. How could she? He's half a man. Not even. Now that her life is back on track, she'll be hanging with the beautiful people again in no time. She'll probably go to the prom with one of the jocks. Justin Wigetaw. Shaheem Dobi. One of those guys with a life and a future and two legs they can stand on.

"Dammit! Dammit! Dammit!" Peter cries, still pummeling himself. He finally collapses forward in exhaustion, bringing his shaking hands to his face. The more he cries, the more pathetic he feels.

What's the point? a little voice in his mind calls out. *Why even bother crying? It's not going to get you anywhere. You're still going to be a vegetable.*

"I can't take this," Peter whispers to himself, the images he'd conjured of him and Meena at the prom over the past few weeks spinning through his mind. Taunting him.

It was all in his grasp and it was snatched away. This has to be a punishment. It has to be. There *is* no point. No point in anything anymore.

There's a light knock on his door and it opens. Peter doesn't look up until the overhead light blazes on and he has to blink against its harsh invasion.

"What?" he spits out when he sees both his parents standing in his doorway.

"We wanted to talk to you about a couple of things, son," his father says, his dark eyes filled with apprehension while his voice booms optimistically like a carnival announcer's.

He exchanges a quick, nervous glance with Peter's mom, and then she takes over. "First, we want you to know we're having some lifts installed on the staircases," she says. "So you'll be able to get upstairs and down to the basement. You can even move back into your old room."

Peter blinks. His parents have purposely avoided making any changes to their living arrangements to accommodate his wheelchair, leaving him stuck on just one floor of the house for months. They seemed so sure that it wasn't worth it—that he'd walk again. But they're convinced now. It's real. He's never getting out of this chair.

When Peter doesn't respond, his father picks up again. "We also wanted to discuss your birthday," he says.

My birthday.

Sirens. Lights. Screams. Gore. Blood.

My birthday . . .

It's going to be even more painful than usual this year.

"We thought we should do something special," his mother adds, lacing her fingers together.

Peter wants to laugh. Something special. Like what? Maybe they should invite the Drivers over to celebrate the anniversary.

Peter looks up at his parents, trying to ascertain, once and for all, if they really are as thick as they seem. Their faces wear matching tentative smiles. They both stand on the other side of the doorway as if they're afraid of being infected by something if they cross the line.

They have no idea what to do with him.

"We could go out. Is there anywhere particular you'd like to go?" his father asks, slipping his hands into his pockets.

"No," Peter answers.

"Think about it, Peter," his mother says, venturing a few small steps into his room. "It's your birthday. We have to do something—even if it's just buy you one of those Carvel cakes you used to love. You know . . . with the little crunchy things?"

She chuckles awkwardly and looks to her husband when Peter doesn't react. Peter's dad shoots her a reassuring glance.

"Come on, son," his father says. "We know it's a very tough time right now, but at least let us take you out to dinner. At least get out of this room."

Peter tips his head forward. It's starting to pound at the temples. They're not going to leave him alone until he agrees— that much is clear. His parents have never been the involved types and he's never seen them this persistent about anything. The word *no* is usually enough to send them packing.

"Fine," he says, solely to make them go away. "Fine, we'll go out to dinner."

You can pretend you're happy to be with me and I can pretend I'm happy to be alive. It'll be a blast.

• • •

When Meena hears the tenth ring on the other end of the phone line on Wednesday afternoon, she gets the feeling that Peter is not going to pick up the phone. She glances across the crowded cafeteria toward the table where Jane, Danny, Reed, Karyn, and Jeremy are all sitting, waiting for her. Waiting for her to be little Miss Party Planner.

How did I get myself into this? she wonders. *What was I thinking?*

"Come on, Peter, pick up," she says under her breath, turning back toward the pay phone.

All the little hairs on the back of her neck are on edge. With every passing second, Meena is more and more certain that Peter didn't get vague news at the doctor on Monday, but that he got the very worst news.

Why won't you talk to me? Meena wonders. *After everything that's happened, why won't you trust me?*

She kicks absently at the cinder block wall until, finally, reluctantly, she gives up and hangs up the phone. Taking a deep breath, Meena glances at the table of Peter's friends once again. Jeremy shoots her a questioning look and Meena forces herself to smile. She holds up one finger and pretends to be busy searching for something in her bag.

Maybe we shouldn't do this, she thinks as she paws through random scraps of paper, pens, an old roll of Life Savers. *If Peter doesn't feel up to school . . . or to talking to me . . . is he really going to be up for a party?*

She knows that a party is the last thing she would have wanted when she was in the depths of her depression over Steven Clayton.

But before she left Peter's house last night, she'd asked Mrs. Davis if she thought the birthday party was still a good idea, and Mrs. Davis had seemed certain. *This is exactly what Peter needs. Go ahead and make the plans.*

And Peter isn't Meena. Maybe a party *is* what he needs. He needs to see how many friends he has. How much support. It doesn't matter to any of them that he's in a wheelchair.

Meena rolls back her shoulders. If there's going to be a party, she's going to make sure it's the best damn party Peter has ever seen.

Meena crosses the room and sinks into an empty chair at the end of the table, pulling out her planning notebook. She feels inexplicably nervous. These people, or most of them, anyway, are . . . were . . . *are* her friends. Maybe she hasn't talked to them in weeks, but that's no reason to be freaked out about talking to them now.

They must be wondering what's been going on with me, Meena thinks, glancing at Karyn, who does have a bit of a questioning look in her eyes. *Why after the weeks of silence and freakishness I've suddenly decided to throw a party.*

But it's for Peter. That other stuff doesn't matter. Not right now.

It doesn't matter that she's going to the police station after school today. That she was up all night, thinking about what she was going to have to say. That if anyone at this table knew what she's been through, they wouldn't even be able to look at her.

Meena takes a deep, shaky breath. *Peter. Think about Peter.*

"Well . . . the birthday boy isn't here today, so at least he can't get suspicious," Meena says.

Everyone laughs quietly. This is weird, all of them sitting here. The last time they all sat together there was a birthday cake with blue icing. A skimpy paper tablecloth with balloons along the rim. There were another two friends. One who is stubbornly not answering the phone. One who never saw another birthday party.

Meena clears her throat. Reed is staring down at the table, in another world. She knows exactly what he's thinking about.

"So! We just need to figure out who's going to get what!" Meena says, forcing herself to sound chipper and hoping it will be contagious.

"Jeremy and I are on music," Danny says, raising his hand slightly. "And . . . uh . . . Cori Lerner's going to lend us her sound system."

"Great," Meena says. "How about decorations?"

"I'll do it," Jane and Karyn say at the same time.

"Well, you can—"

"No . . . if you want to—"

"Why don't the three of us go?" Reed suggests. "We can hit that party store over on 19."

Meena glances at Karyn, who flushes inexplicably, and she notices Jane looking back and forth at Karyn and Reed as well. Meena has less than no clue what's going on between the two of them. It's bizarre. She used to get all the gossip.

"I get a discount there," Karyn puts in. "You know . . . cheerleading."

"So you and Reed should go," Jane says amicably.

"No!" Karyn says, then flushes in unison with Reed. Karyn laughs a slight, uncomfortable laugh. "No, Jane, you should come, too. I mean, I always buy the same stuff because I'm in there all the time. It would be good to have another girl's opinion."

"So we're settled, then," Reed says, turning to look Karyn directly in the eye. "The three of us will go."

"Okay!" Meena says, trying to get past whatever this weirdness is. "You guys are on decorations." She draws in her notebook. Hearts. Swirls. Jagged lines.

"I guess I can do food," Danny says, leaning forward. "If we're going on expertise, junk food is mine."

More laughter. That's better. Meena smiles as she looks down at her list of things to do. If Peter could only see this. If he could only see what everyone is doing for him.

"Okay, then . . . all I really need is a head count," Meena says.

"Got it!" Danny says. He pulls a folded piece of loose-leaf paper out of his back pocket and hands it over. "Looks like it'll be a good turnout."

Meena unfolds the page and looks over Danny's chicken scratch. There are drawings all along the edges of the page—party hats, silly drunken partyers, little cakes and presents. Meena feels her heart give a little flutter. It looks like everyone is coming. Peter has more people that care about him than he knows.

It's going to be okay, Meena thinks as the others fall into conversations about the music and exactly how many bags of chips Jeremy needs to get. *Once Peter sees all his friends together, he's going to be okay.*

• • •

She was flirting with me. She was definitely flirting with me, Reed thinks as he turns onto his block late on Wednesday evening. He feels a smile start to spread across his face and he forces his mouth into a straight line.

"No, she wasn't," he says, reaching over to turn the music up. "She was just being Karyn."

Reed takes a deep breath and tries to concentrate on driving. But he's just spent an hour shopping with Karyn and Jane and it was among the sixty most confusing minutes of his life. Karyn had touched his arm a few times. She'd giggled. She'd definitely said he was cute when he suggested WWF plates and napkins. But she'd also caught herself a few times. She looked away right after the cute comment. And at one point, when she was going to touch him, she'd quickly changed course and pretended she was going for a centerpiece on the shelf behind him.

Unfortunately for her, the centerpiece had turned out to be a Star of David. Not the most convincing cover.

"Forget about her," Reed tells himself. "You are just going to be friends."

It sounds good. It's just too bad his heart doesn't seem to be listening.

As he approaches his house, all Reed can think about is putting on some sweats and vegging in front of the TV, but the second he pulls into the driveway, all hopes of a relaxing evening are obliterated.

T. J.'s SUV is in the garage. Reed puts the car in park

and lowers his head to the steering wheel. This is all he needs. Another screaming match with T. J. The perfect end to a messed-up day.

"Why did Jeremy have to move home this week?" Reed mutters aloud. He's happy that Jeremy worked things out with his family but has to admit, he misses the guy. It was nice having an ally in this house.

As he turns off the engine and pops open the door, another, more hopeful thought hits Reed. Maybe T. J. isn't here to fight. Maybe he's thought it over and he's ready to forgive Reed.

He shakes his head and laughs at himself. That is beyond impossible. But maybe . . . just maybe T. J. is ready to talk. Or listen. Or *something*. Reed has to hold on to that something.

He pulls his backpack and duffel bag out of the car and heads for the house, keeping the little flame of hope alive—until the moment he walks through the door. Then all hope is forgotten and replaced by stunned confusion. The foyer is filled with bags, crates, boxes. T. J.'s TV sits in the corner facing the wall with a stack of textbooks piled on top of it. There's a huge garbage bag filled with balled-up clothes.

Before Reed can take it all in, his mother enters the foyer from the kitchen. She's so intent on staring at the floor, she doesn't even see Reed.

"Mom?" he says.

She looks up. Her face is pale and there are dried tears

on her cheeks. Reed's heart instantly goes out to her.

"What's going on?" he asks, clutching his own bags.

"I think you should talk to your brother," she says flatly. "I'm washing my hands of this whole mess." She turns and places one foot on the stairs, then stops and slowly faces him again. "The only thing I *will* say is that brothers shouldn't treat each other this way. They shouldn't let this kind of thing happen. Especially not brothers who love each other. Who have *always* loved each other."

Then she jogs up the stairs and disappears into her room. Reed just hovers there for a moment, feeling like he's walked into someone else's house. Someone else's family argument. Everything is alien to him lately. His family has a whole new brand of dysfunction.

Taking each step deliberately, Reed climbs the stairs and walks down the hall, going directly to his brother's room. The door is open. T. J. is hanging his Nerf basketball net on the back of his closet door.

"What're you doing?" Reed asks, sounding like a five-year-old version of himself—small. Stupid. Afraid of the answer.

"What's it look like I'm doing?" T. J. asks, picking up a foam ball from his bed and swishing it through the hoop. "I'm dropping out."

• • •

Jane slips through the front door of her house and shuts it as quietly as possible behind her. There are voices coming from the kitchen. She knows her father is here because his car is sitting in the driveway, the engine still clicking like it's just been turned off. What she doesn't know is *why* he's here.

And not knowing that is creating major knots in her shoulder muscles.

She tiptoes over to the kitchen door and peeks inside, then blinks. Her mother is setting the kitchen table while her father stirs—from the smell of it—a pot of mushroom gravy on the stove.

Has she gone back in time to kindergarten? That's the last time she recalls witnessing such a serene scenario between her parents.

"Uh . . . hi?" Jane says, stepping tentatively into the room.

"Hi, Janie," her father says, turning away from the stove briefly.

"How was your day?" her mother asks as she leans across the table to place a fork and knife next to a plate. She crosses her arms and looks at Jane expectantly.

A jolt of trepidation skitters down Jane's spine. *Here we go!* she thinks. They'll start with, "How was your day?" then move on to, "Did you get any tests back?" "Did you practice this morning?" "Where have you been all afternoon?"

"It was good," Jane says, hovering by the door and leaving her jacket on. She may need to make a quick getaway. "I went shopping with Reed Frasier and Karyn Aufiero just now. We're having a birthday party for Peter Davis this weekend."

That's where I've been all afternoon, she adds silently, happy that she's headed them off at the pass.

Jane's parents exchange a curious, somewhat disturbed look when they hear the words *Peter Davis* and *birthday party* in the same sentence. Jane bites her lip and looks at the floor, her heart swelling painfully.

"That's nice," her father says finally.

Jane glances at his broad back as he stoops slightly over the stove. "Dad, don't take this the wrong way, but what are you doing here?"

Her father chuckles, but it's her mother who answers. "We just thought that after all the insanity lately it would be nice to prove that we're all capable of sitting down together and having a nice meal."

"Oh," Jane says, allowing herself to relax a bit, even though the situation still feels suspect. These two have never felt the need to prove they could be civil before, since their very uncivil divorce.

Still, Jane pulls off her jacket and lays it down on the chair at the end of the table, then takes her seat along the side. Her father brings the mushroom sauce over to the table as her mother puts the last of the food on trivets scattered over the surface.

"It smells great," Jane says, looking at them for any

signs of an attack. But her mother is simply breaking open a roll while her father dishes up potatoes.

"So, Jane, how's the studying going?" her father asks as he slaps a spoonful of white rice onto her plate.

There it is! Jane thinks.

"Dad—"

"No pressure!" he says, holding up the spoon in surrender. "I'm just asking. I want to know how you're doing."

Narrowing her eyes, Jane decides to give him the benefit of the doubt. "The studying is fine," she says, unfolding her napkin into her lap. "Quinn has really been helping."

"So you find that useful—studying with a friend?" her mother asks.

Jane looks at her. What is her angle? There has to be an angle, doesn't there? If she answers yes, her mother will say, "But you must end up wasting some valuable time with someone there to distract you." If she answers no, her father will say, "Then why bother? Why are you wasting time with this guy?"

As her pulse starts to race, Jane's parents wait for an answer, watching her expectantly. She's stuck. She's caught. They've got her. How did they get so good?

"Yes. I do," she blurts finally, clenching her fists to steel herself for battle.

"That's great," her father says with a nod. "It's good that you have someone who's . . . recently gone through the same things. Testing . . . applying . . ."

Jane's mouth starts to fall open. There's no way he just said that. Are these people actually listening to her? Actually being supportive? Something is not right here. She feels like she's being watched. Like someone's filming with hidden cameras.

That's it! Jane thinks wildly. *Any second now some cheesy TV host is going to walk in from the patio and tell me they've replaced my parents with cyborgs.*

"So . . . how did it go with your advisers?" her mother asks, taking a bite of chicken. "Did they give you a hard time when you dropped your clubs?"

"Some of them," Jane answers, still trying to accept the fact that they're having an actual conversation. "But it was okay."

"Good," her mother says with a stiff smile. "That's . . . good."

Jane can tell that her mother wants to say something more. Is undoubtedly dying to try to talk her into rejoining the volunteer band or something, but she just returns to her meal. It takes some obvious effort, but she does it.

Smiling to herself, Jane digs into her own dinner for the first time. Her parents may not be perfect, but they're trying. They're listening and they're trying. Jane can't imagine asking for more.

● ● ●

"Peter! Meena's on the phone again! Do you want to talk to her?"

His mother's voice is so loud and piercing, it startles him even through two rooms and his closed bedroom door.

"No!" he shouts back, his head pounding. "I didn't want to talk to her last time, why would I want to talk to her this time?" he adds under his breath.

His chair is parked in front of the end table next to his bed, facing the television, which is dark and silent. The only light in the room comes from the lame, low-watt lightbulb in the desk lamp across the room. In the last hour or so, Peter has absently thought of moving himself to his bed about a hundred times, but he doesn't have the energy to do it. What's the point?

The phone rings again and Peter rolls his eyes, then squeezes them shut.

"Peter! It's Danny!"

"No!" he shouts again.

Why doesn't his mother just leave him alone? Why don't they *all* just leave him alone? All he wants is to sit here in the dark and quiet—is that too much to ask? But maybe it is. No one cares about what he wants. And why should they?

Peter reaches down into the pocket on his wheelchair and shakily pulls out the crumpled photo of him and his friends from his tenth birthday. There's a white crease down the center of his forehead and another one slicing across Karyn's mouth, making her smile look obscenely wide and maniacal. Everyone else is distorted and bumpy.

But they still look happy. Innocent. Clueless.

If only they'd known what was going to happen. If only they'd known that in a little over an hour from the time this picture was taken, their lives were going to change forever.

"And they've only gotten worse," Peter says, his eyes gazing down at Meena's little face.

All that pain. All that pain they've each gone through at the hands of someone they thought they could trust. Parents. Friends. Boyfriends. Girlfriends. Brothers. Sisters. Doctors. Teachers. What is the point of living when so much can happen to you? So much over which you have no control.

Peter runs his fingertip over the rough surface of the photograph. Maybe it all could have been prevented. Maybe if that day had turned out differently—if he hadn't done what he'd done—maybe they'd all be happy now. Maybe none of them would have ended up on the painful paths they've taken.

It's all his fault. They've all been through so much and it's all Peter's fault.

Witnessing that kind of tragedy . . . it does something to little kids. Changes them in a fundamental way. Peter watched enough talk shows when he was in the hospital after the accident to know that. Maybe if they hadn't seen what they saw that day, they never would have let themselves be taken advantage of by their parents, their siblings, their friends and teachers. Maybe they'd all be happy, well-adjusted people.

It's all my fault, Peter tells himself. *It's all my fault.*

He crumples the photo once more and lets it fall into the pocket again. He can't look at it anymore. Can't see what the people he cares about used to be.

I'm worthless. All I do is cause pain to the people around me. I'm just crowding up the earth in my stupid wheelchair. Just wasting space.

He brings his hands to his face and knows he should be crying, but he can't. The tears won't come. His body has accepted it and his mind is just now catching up. He's done here. He never should have been here.

This birthday is going to be his last.

Taking a deep breath, Peter looks up, filled with a sense of purpose.

He knows where the gun is. He's always known. All he has to do is get it. He has two whole days to prepare himself.

This Friday he'll turn seventeen and then he'll take his own life. Exactly seven years to the day. It will be poetic justice.

CHAPTER SEVEN

"Mom, Dad?" Meena calls out as she walks into her house on Thursday afternoon, her heart already doing its shallow, rapidly beating dance of fear. It's the middle of the afternoon and their cars are outside. Both of them are here . . . somewhere. Something must have happened.

Meena's mind flashes on the police station. The small, clean, orange-and-white room they'd sat her down in the day before. The pretty, kinky-haired female officer that had taken her statement. The little coffee spot on the woman's blouse Meena had stared at as she spoke. Random images and words and smells have been haunting her all day long.

"Meena!"

Her mother emerges from the kitchen, wiping her hands on a plaid dish towel. She seems fine—a little bit pale, but otherwise fine. She takes one look at Meena's face and her own features soften with sympathy.

"Everything's okay, honey," she says. "Come into the kitchen. Your dad and I want to talk to you."

Meena takes a deep breath, but she's not completely convinced by her mother's assurance. *Something must have happened with Steven,* she thinks, following her mom into the kitchen. The officer had been kind, sympathetic. But she had also wanted every detail.

It was like living the whole rape over again. In front of a stranger. In front of her parents.

What if she didn't believe me? Meena wonders, her mind starting to race. *What if the police told Steven he'd been accused and they all had a good laugh over it? "That poor disillusioned little girl . . ."*

She swallows hard, trying to keep herself from getting sick, and steps into the kitchen.

Her father is seated at a stool next to the island in the middle of the room. He looks up and gives her a thin smile as she walks in.

"What's going on?" Meena asks, shrugging out of her jacket. She falls onto a stool, already shaky from the suspense. "What happened?"

The coffee stain . . . the lights . . . the chubby guy behind the desk, looking at her quizzically as she waited . . . the vending machine . . . the rape crisis pamphlets . . . the tangerine-colored upholstery . . .

Was it for nothing? Had she done it all for nothing?

Her mother and father exchange a look and then her father turns back to her. "Steven was arrested this afternoon," he says.

Meena's heart drops. She's not sure why. This is what she's been expecting . . . even hoping for . . . right? So why does she suddenly feel more scared than ever?

Before she has time to realize it, Meena bursts into tears. Her brain, her heart, her soul are crowded with conflicting emotions and they all seem to want to get out through sobs as quickly as possible.

When did they do it . . . ? Was he scared . . . ? Does he hate me . . . ?

Who cares! *He's behind bars! He'll be punished! He's being punished! He deserves it!*

But what if he makes bail? What if he comes after me? What about Lydia and Trace . . . ?

Her mother is hugging her, but Meena can't even get up the energy to hug her back. It's too much. It's all just too much.

"Everything's going to be okay now," her mother says, kissing the top of her head. "You don't have anything to worry about anymore, sweetie."

Meena turns her face and buries it in her mother's thick wool sweater. She wants to stop crying. Wants to be that strong person, but she can't even seem to catch her breath. It's a few minutes before her sobs finally subside and eventually quiet altogether. She sniffles loudly and pulls away from her mom, wiping under her nose with the back of her hand.

"Are you okay?" her father asks, reaching out to touch her arm.

Meena's eyes are so swollen, they feel the size of golf balls. Her father is all blurry when she looks at him.

"Sorry," she says, grabbing a napkin from the little pile on the island. She dabs at her eyes with the coarse paper. "I guess I kind of exploded."

"It's fine," her father says, giving her arm a squeeze. "You can explode whenever you want to."

Meena lets out a small laugh and blows her nose into the napkin. *Steven was arrested,* she thinks, letting the fact finally sink in.

"Speaking of exploding . . . ," her mother says slowly. She reaches out and touches Meena's face with both hands, then pulls back again, the swipe of her fingers sending a pleasant warmth over Meena's skin. "Meena, we don't need to discuss this now, but we really think you need to tell Dr. Lansky what happened to you."

Meena looks at the floor. More stomach turns. Tell someone else? They want her to tell someone else?

"We know it's hard, sweetie, but he's there to help you," her mother continues. "He's there to help you deal with this."

Help me deal . . . Meena doesn't need someone to help her deal with this. She has someone. Or at least she did until recently. She has Peter.

Suddenly all she wants to do is tell him the news.

"Meena? Will you at least think about it?" her father asks.

"Yeah, Dad," Meena says quickly. "I will."

She knows they're right. That Dr. Lansky probably will

be able to help her deal with things no one else could ever help her with. And she will think about telling him. But for now, she's practically aching to talk to someone else.

"I'm gonna go make a phone call," Meena says, sliding off the stool.

"Okay," her mother says, reaching out to push Meena's hair away from her face. "We'll be here when you're done."

Meena takes her jacket and her bag and trudges up to her room, her body feeling heavier than a sumo wrestler's. She drops onto her bed and picks up the phone, automatically dialing Peter's number. She knows he won't answer, but maybe there's a chance. And after everything he's done for her, he deserves to know what's going on.

Meena lifts the phone to her ear and is greeted by the piercing sound of a busy signal. She sniffles and hangs up, then lies back into her pillows. Every day that passes that she doesn't talk to Peter makes it feel like he's another hundred miles away from her. A few weeks ago she barely knew him, and now she can't stand not knowing what's going on in his head. Not being able to tell him what's going on in hers.

Maybe he'll be in school tomorrow and we can talk then, she thinks, trying to make herself believe it. And if not, there's always his party tomorrow night. Not that she's going to bring up the subject of Steven Clayton then.

But at least she'll see Peter. At least she'll know for sure that he's okay.

• • •

"So, Danny, how are the new meds?" Dr. Lansky asks on Thursday afternoon. "Have you been keeping track of any side effects?"

"You bet," Danny says with a nod. He pulls his spiral notebook out of his backpack and hands it over. "I wrote down the times of the lows and how long they lasted," he explains.

Danny feels almost proud of himself for completing the task. He's never done anything his therapist has told him to do before. In the past, Danny has always taken the I'm-not-a-lab-rat stance on projects like this. But he's actually been feeling better lately. And if writing this stuff down will get the illustrious doctor to mess with his dosage again and make him feel even *better*, Danny's in. He'll do whatever he can.

At least that's how he feels about it today.

"This looks good, Danny," Dr. Lansky says, nodding as he flips through the notebook. "You're having fewer lows, I see."

"Yeah, but they still suck," Danny says bluntly.

Lansky chuckles and closes the book, laying it aside. "I'm sure they do," he says, adjusting his legs and making a note in the steno pad he has perpetually perched on his thigh. "We'll discuss that at the end of your session. But for now, I'd just like to hear how things are going. School . . . family . . . friends . . . ?"

Danny can tell that Dr. Lansky half expects him not to answer his question. His pen is poised, but there's a doubtful look in his eye. Probably because most days he comes here, Danny just sits on the couch and says next to nothing for an entire hour—a feat that takes real patience for a person with as much to say as Danny.

"Things are okay," Danny says, picking at his thumbnail. "My family is still watching me like I'm some kind of freak show, though."

"Why do you think that is?" Lansky asks.

"Because I *am* a freak show," Danny replies. He crosses his arms over his chest. "I get it, though, I do. They don't want me to do something dangerous again."

"And you?"

"And me, what?" Danny asks, letting his discomfort come out in a flash of anger. "I don't want to do anything dangerous again, either."

"Good," Lansky says, making a note. What Danny wouldn't give for one good look in that book. "So how about friends? Any girls in the picture?"

The smile lights Danny's face before he can squelch it. Dr. Lansky's gray eyebrows pop up and Danny looks away, blushing slightly.

"Tell me about her," Dr. Lansky says.

Danny takes a deep breath. Part of him doesn't want to share Cori with this guy. He's spent the last couple of months resenting this touchy-feely ooey-gooey doctor and Danny doesn't want to get all sharey with him now. He'd feel like a wuss. Like he was caving in.

But talking about Cori is one of his favorite things to do, besides actually *being* with her. And it will definitely make the hour pass a hell of a lot faster than sitting here in silence.

"Her name's Cori and she's perfect," Danny begins. Dr. Lansky leans back in his chair with a studious expression on his face. This must be making his day—getting actual insight into Danny Chaiken. "We were friends first and then we started hanging out more. . . ."

Within a few minutes, Danny finds himself having an actual conversation with Dr. Lansky. He even laughs once or twice. Lansky has a sense of humor when given the opportunity. Danny doesn't even mind—in fact, barely notices—when the conversation flips to the subject of his parents and their trust.

I can do this, Danny thinks as Dr. Lansky scribbles into his pad. *I can actually do this.* He's still not convinced that these heart-to-hearts are going to actually change anything, but the mere fact that the hour is flying by is enough to get him almost giddy.

"You seem to be doing much better," Dr. Lansky says with a smile.

Yeah, Danny thinks, his heart swelling with a bit of pride. Things are changing. In a good way. And he *should* be proud of that. He shouldn't feel like he's giving in.

"I guess I am," he says with a smile.

• • •

Jane feels a bit out of place as she walks into Karyn's

119

house on Thursday afternoon. She holds her grocery bags close to her chest as she walks along the hallway, not wanting to touch anything. Like a little kid in a museum. Not that the place is pristine and beautiful—it's actually kind of disheveled and homey. But Jane hasn't stepped foot in Karyn Aufiero's house since grade school.

Karyn, however, seems to think having Jane over is as everyday an experience as cheerleading practice.

"Just dump the bags on the counter," Karyn says breezily as they walk into the kitchen. Karyn flicks on the lights and turns on the oven to preheat. "What should we bake first? I think chocolate chip because then we can eat them while we make the other stuff."

Jane laughs and puts down her things. "Sounds good to me," she says. "So, why did you feel the need to bake again?"

Karyn shrugs. "I know Danny and Jeremy are gonna get the standard chips and pretzels and stuff, but I thought it would be nice to have a personal touch, you know? Just call me Martha. I've done this for a ton of cheerleading bake sales, so it's second nature by now."

They unpack the groceries and Karyn starts to pull the necessary tools out of the cabinets and drawers—bowls, measuring cups, spoons. Jane watches her, wondering if Karyn thinks this is half as strange as she does—Jane Scott and Karyn Aufiero, getting together to bake for Peter Davis's birthday party. It's like something off the Sci Fi Channel.

Jane's about to mention it, but then she realizes that if she does, she'll look like a tremendous dork.

Karyn is one of the popular people, moving in that realm and, until recently, never really looking outside it. Jane has never thought that Karyn is a bad person, just sort of . . . elite.

Still, Karyn did invite her over here. And yesterday they'd had a few laughs while shopping with Reed. Jane decides she might as well try to get to know the girl again. If Peter and Reed like her, she has to be fairly cool.

"So, Karyn, how's your life?" she asks as she slips out of her wool coat.

Karyn laughs. "It's fine, thank you," she says.

"No more homicidal tendencies with your friends?" Jane asks.

"Not recently," Karyn replies. She dumps a couple of sticks of butter into a bowl and starts mashing them. "I don't know . . . things are . . . weird, actually. Good, but weird."

"What do you mean?" Jane asks.

She pulls the canister of flour toward her and starts measuring, making a complete mess. Jane can't remember the last time she baked anything, but from the way Karyn is flitting around the kitchen, it seems like she's a pro.

"Well . . . I'm alone for the first time ever, basically," Karyn says, picking up an egg. "I mean, I broke up with T. J." She pauses and looks across the room as if she's trying to let the fact sink in. "I broke up with T. J. It's so weird."

"Do you miss him?" Jane asks, quickly swiping the

excess flour into her hand before Karyn sees what a spaz she is.

"I do . . . but it's not that," Karyn says. "This is gonna sound weird, but I kind of like being alone. I mean, it's scary, but it's also kind of . . . freeing, I guess."

She looks at Jane, her blue eyes narrowing. "Is that totally bizarre?" she asks, clearly embarrassed.

Jane smiles. "No, it's really not," she says. "I kind of know what you mean. Not the guy thing, but the free thing."

"Yeah?" Karyn asks, cracking the egg expertly into the bowl. She picks up a wooden spoon and starts to stir like a madwoman.

"Well, for the first time in my life my parents aren't on top of me all the time," Jane says. "It's amazing, you know? Not having them looking over my shoulder, asking me what I'm doing every second of the day. It's like, I'm seventeen and I actually know what freedom feels like."

Karyn stops her crazy stirring and looks up at Jane, an almost devilish smile playing about her lips. "It's kind of great, isn't it?" she asks.

Jane grins right back, her heart warming and her whole body relaxing for the first time since she walked through the door. Karyn Aufiero *is* actually fairly cool.

"Yeah," Jane answers. "It kind of is."

• • •

I'm going to get him to talk to me, Reed thinks, wiping his clammy hands on his jeans as he hovers outside the door to the den on Thursday night. T. J. is inside, watching

122

a *Friends* rerun. Reed hasn't seen T. J. yet, but he *knows* it's not his mother in there watching Ross and Rachel duke it out for the four-hundredth time. *I don't even care if it's just a "hello." At least then I'd be getting somewhere.*

He takes a deep breath and clenches his fists, then steps into the dimly lit den. He's just opening his mouth when T. J. picks up the remote, flicks off the TV, and storms toward the door on the other side of the room.

A blast of heat covers Reed's face and races through his body. He can't take this anymore. He can't live here with T. J. if he's going to be treated like this. Before long, *Reed* is going to be moving in with *Jeremy's* family.

"God, T. J., would you stop acting like such a baby?" Reed spits out before T. J. can make it out into the hallway.

T. J. stops short and reels around. Reed almost takes a step back. The vein in his brother's forehead is so obvious, it looks like a map of the Mississippi.

"*I'm* acting like a baby?" T. J. shouts, pointing his beefy hand at his even beefier chest. "Look who's talking, *little* brother." He takes a few steps back into the room. His whole body seems to be swelling with tension and his arms are suspended a few inches away from his body like a pro wrestler's. Like he's ready to throw down. "Do you have to take everything I have? Did you have to take the *only* thing I had?"

I tried to take Karyn, too, but that didn't quite work, a sarcastic voice in Reed's head pipes up.

"You know, when I went back to school on Monday, I

123

went directly to the athletic office and asked them what the hell was going on," T. J. fumes. "Sure enough, they tell me they're keeping me second string and my kid brother is going to be the starter. Do you have any idea how humiliating that was? Mom's all asking me, 'Why did you have to drop out? Why did you have to drop out?'" He makes his voice whiny and high-pitched to mimic their mother. "But how was I supposed to stay there after that?"

T. J. pauses for air and Reed crosses his arms over his chest, trying to think of the right thing to say.

You could play second string, he thinks. *Go to school with me and have fun and play football together like we always have. Who cares who's first and who's second?*

But he knows his brother doesn't think that way. His brother has never been anything but first.

"I didn't do this on purpose," Reed says finally. "They came to me."

"So what? So you have to say yes?" T. J. asks, his voice returning to a more normal volume. His eyes are almost pleading and Reed has to look away. "Reed, you can be anything you want. You're the brain. You could be a lawyer or a doctor or some Wall Street trader guy. But all I've got is football. That's it, man. And you took it away."

"Look, I'm sorry—"

"Save it," T. J. says. "All you care about is yourself."

As soon as Reed hears those words, something inside him snaps. How could T. J. say that? How could anyone think of Reed that way? All he's done his entire life is sit back and watch while T. J. was lauded by coaches and reporters and scouts. While their mother polished his trophies and shoved Reed's academic awards in a drawer. He's let T. J. have the spotlight as long as he can remember. And not just that. He's let their mother believe that T. J. was the perfect son. Always covering for him when he broke curfew, doing T. J.'s chores, picking up after him. And for what? So *he* can be thought of as *selfish?*

"Me?" Reed says, barely able to control his voice. "All *I* care about is *myself?* Are you kidding me? Do you know what it's like to hear Mom brag about you to everyone? To have her not so much as mention me when her friends ask how the family is? To always have to wear your hand-me-downs and drive the crappy car and have the smaller room and do all your stupid chores?"

T. J.'s face scrunches up in disbelief. Like he can't even imagine what Reed is talking about.

Reed has to get out of this room. If he doesn't, he's going to lose it completely.

"T. J., I'm sorry you took the worst of it from Dad, all right? But I've been paying you back for it my whole life," Reed says, struggling to hold back the full force of his anger. "And you have to wake up and realize that I haven't taken anything from you. Those guys at BC didn't think you were good enough. If I hadn't taken the spot, they would have given it to somebody else."

All the blood rushes out of T. J.'s face and for a moment, Reed thinks his brother is going to throw up. But even that doesn't stop his tirade.

"That's the way it is, T. J., and I can't change it. And I'm not going to take responsibility for it, either," Reed says. "And you know what? Mom's right. You didn't have to drop out. You're the one who gave up. I didn't make you. And I'm not going to feel guilty because you screwed yourself over. I'm just not."

Reed turns and stalks out of the room before his emotions can completely overwhelm him. He rushes up to his room and slams the door behind him, struggling for a good, deep breath. Struggling to keep from crying.

Then he hears the door open behind him and he whirls around, expecting to see T. J. ready to lunge at him. Instead his mother stands there, looking up at him, her eyes wide with sorrow and a twinge of fear. His fists unclench, but only slightly.

She's probably worried I've done something else to her precious T. J., Reed thinks.

"What, Mom?" Reed blurts out, not caring about the hostility in his voice.

She blinks, then turns to close the door behind her. "I . . . uh . . . I heard you boys fighting," she says, rubbing her delicate hands together as if she's trying to warm them.

"Yeah," Reed says, lowering himself onto the end of his bed and bracing his arms behind him.

"Reed, we've all been through a lot . . . ," she says.

This is the part where she tells me that it's so much harder on T. J. He has dyslexia. He took the brunt of it. I should be kind to my brother.

"But I think I never . . . I think I never thought of you in relation to—"

"Mom," Reed interrupts, wanting to get this over with. "What are you trying to say?"

She pulls up straight and looks at him and for the first time he sees that there are tears in her eyes.

"I'm sorry," she says. "What I'm trying to say is that I never realized how much everything affected you. You've always been so strong and so smart and so together." She looks away and takes in a shaky breath, giving Reed a moment to absorb what she has just said.

Strong . . . smart . . . together. Is that how she really thinks of him?

"I suppose I always just thought you were too young," she continues, gazing at the picture of him and T. J. that sits on his desk. "That what . . . what your father did couldn't have affected you because you were too young."

Reed swallows hard, his heart twisting painfully. He was very young. But not too young to understand. Not too young to hurt. Not too young to be petrified of his own father. He clasps his hands together in his lap and looks down at the floor, the tears welling up all over again.

"I know it doesn't mean much right now," she says.

"But I want you to know . . . I want you to know that I love you, Reed."

Reed brings his hands to his face as the tears break free. He tries his best to be quiet. To not shake. The effort is almost too much.

Don't do it! his mind screams. *Don't cry in front of her!*

"I should go," she says.

He hears the door open and click quietly closed and he lets it all out. Cries for real. His mother has no idea. Not a clue in the world.

But she's right about one thing—what she's just said doesn't mean much. It means everything.

● ● ●

The moment his digital clock switches over from 12:59 to 1:00 A.M. in the wee hours of Peter's birthday, he pushes his blankets away from his legs and sits up. He struggles into his wheelchair and opens the door of his room. His parents are asleep upstairs. The house is deathly quiet.

He wheels himself down the hallway and over to the front door. He's not nervous about getting caught. Not scared about going outside alone in his chair in the middle of the night. He's not feeling much of anything these days. He knows what he has to do, and he's doing it.

The front door squeaks quietly as it opens but not enough to wake the lightest of sleepers. Peter wheels himself outside, closes the door behind him, and starts down the ramp. It's made of a bright, yellow wood that contrasts sharply with the gray paint on the deck, and it still smells pungently like it's just been cut.

What will they do with it when he's gone? Will they have it taken away, or will they leave it there to remind them of him? Will they leave it there out of sheer laziness?

The door to the garage protests a bit more loudly than the front door had, but Peter is soon inside. It's dark as pitch and colder than an icebox. Peter reaches up and flicks on the light, then blinks against its blinding effects. The room is lined with shelves displaying more junk than any family should legally be allowed to preserve. His father's old motorcycle stands against the far wall, rotting away unused. Peter remembers when he was very little and his dad used to take him out on slow rides around the neighborhood. Peter couldn't wait for the day when he could ride it on his own. Be big and cool and swagger like his father.

But the older Peter got, the clearer it became that his father wasn't actually cool and, in fact, had no swagger. And now there's no chance Peter's ever going to ride that bike.

Peter forces himself to focus on the red metal shelving unit directly across from him. *You're here for a reason.*

He pushes his way across the cement floor and lines himself up next to the shelves.

It's there. It's right there, he thinks. On the shelf just a foot away from him—just at eye level—is a blue milk crate filled with dirty, oil-stained rags. But Peter knows there's something else in that crate. He's known it for a long time.

Breathing slowly, deliberately, to keep his pulse from racing, Peter reaches forward and pulls the crate toward him, letting it fall into his lap. He doesn't feel a thing.

He inhales the pungent scent of motor oil and starts to remove the rags, one by one, until the crate is completely empty. Completely empty, that is, except for the gun case lying neatly at the bottom.

Why did he keep it? Peter wonders, staring down at the plain black case. He thought it would affect him more than it does. He thought he'd feel scared, sad, angry, but he doesn't. He just feels mildly curious.

His father had taken a lot of heat down at the station once everyone found out what had happened. The gun had gone into evidence and none of his father's colleagues had let it drop. What was a police officer doing with a gun in the house in a place that was accessible to children? Why would he keep bullets nearby? What kind of parent was he?

Peter reaches into the crate and picks up the case, then places the crate back on the shelf for the moment. Even though his father had been humiliated, even though he'd been depressed for months, for some reason he'd kept the gun after it had been returned. After the incident had been declared an accident. *Why?*

"Maybe he wanted to keep it as a reminder," Peter says quietly, running his hand over the smooth surface of the case. *A reminder of what could go wrong.*

Peter places the case on his thighs and pops it open. The

gun gleams in the fluorescent light. He can't believe he's actually looking at it. Actually holding it. After all this time of pretending that he didn't know where his father hid the thing, here he is in the middle of the night, holding it in his hands.

There are no bullets in the case, but that's not a problem. Peter's father had conscientiously locked up his police-issue gun and ammo for years, but he's become more lax of late.

Peter knows exactly where the bullets are.

As Peter takes the gun out and slips it into the pocket on the side of his wheelchair, he thinks of his father. Of how depressed he was back then. Of how hard he took the fact that his son was responsible.

Maybe after tomorrow night, that depression will finally be completely gone. He'll no longer have to look at Peter. He'll no longer have to remember his humiliation. He'll no longer have to be disappointed.

Peter replaces the empty case in the crate and piles the rags on top of it, then places the crate back on the shelf.

I'm doing the right thing, he tells himself as he makes his way across the garage again. *None of my so-called friends will miss me. They all have good lives going now. And I'm just dead-weight to my parents. They'll be much happier without me.*

One last dinner. He is going to have one last birthday dinner with his parents tomorrow night. And as soon as he gets home, it'll all be over.

CHAPTER EiGHT

"We have to be ready by the time they get home from dinner," Meena tells the rest of the party setup crew as they walk into Peter's house on Friday night. She holds the door open as Reed, Jeremy, Jane, Karyn, Danny, and Cori slip through, carrying bags of food and decorations, stereo equipment, and a huge crate filled with CDs.

Meena is practically shaking with nerves. Aside from the sick tension of being back at Peter's house for a birthday party, she's also being social—really social—for the first time in weeks. She can't remember the last time she hung out with this many people outside of school. And she keeps waiting for someone to ask her why she's been a walking zombie since October. Luckily, though, they all have something much bigger on their minds tonight.

"When are they getting back?" Karyn asks as she walks by Meena.

"Uh . . . around eight," Meena says.

She closes the door and they all stand there. Crowded

together. No one speaks. No one moves. The house might as well be haunted.

"Where's the basement?" Cori asks, like it's a perfectly normal question.

Meena's heart flutters nervously. She glances at Jeremy and sees his jaw tighten. Karyn shifts her weight from one foot to the other. Danny looks at his shoes. Jane glances around behind her as if she's checking out the house.

"What?" Cori asks. So innocent and clueless. Meena almost forgot that not everyone in the world has the same dread of the Davis basement that she and the other five people in the room have.

"It's over here," Reed says.

His posture is ramrod straight as he turns on the heel of his sneaker and walks toward the kitchen. The white wooden door to the basement is just to the right once they're through the kitchen door. Reed stops with his hand on the doorknob and looks at Meena. All she can think is that she's glad it's not her hand on that doorknob. She's not the one that has to do it. She's not the one who's about to open the door to her nightmares.

Reed takes a deep breath, turns the knob, and pulls. Meena half expects the door to creak loudly like every door in every scary movie ever made, but it doesn't. It opens smoothly. Noiselessly. As if it doesn't know its place in the world.

The first thing Meena sees is the wheelchair lift, so recently installed, no one has had time to repaint around it.

Suddenly Reed seems to lose his nerve. He stands aside, waiting for someone else to go first. Meena clears her throat, swallows her fears, and brushes by him. He shoots her a thankful glance as her foot hits the first stair.

It's pitch-black down below, but as soon as Meena gets one whiff of the musty basement smell, she swirls back in time. Suddenly she can see the basement with stunning clarity. Just the way it was the last time she saw it. Wood paneling. Flat gray carpeting with multicolored flecks. A TV so old, it doesn't have a remote. A Ping-Pong table with a sagging net. A fraying, tan couch.

The closet.

The closet with the sliding door that folds in the middle. The wood that's painted white. The paint cracking.

And the people. All the people. She and Karyn and Jane huddled in the corner, waiting for their parents. A skinny, bucktoothed EMT hovering over a white sheet. Peter's father fighting with a paunchy policeman, telling him not to bother the girls. Not until their parents get here.

Meena reaches for the light switch, shaking. She doesn't want to see it. If the smell is enough to do this to her, imagine what seeing it will do. She pauses. Considers turning and running out of the house. But she can't. There are six people behind her, waiting for her to do what needs to be done.

Meena flicks the light switch. The overhead lights blaze on. The basement looks completely, utterly different.

Sigh of relief. Meena descends the stairs and steps onto

plush blue carpeting. Looks around at bright white walls with ugly, but somehow comforting paintings of fruit and flowers hung along them. An old blue and gray living-room set—couch, chair, love seat—sits in the right side of the room in front of a big-screen TV. The Ping-Pong table is still there, but it's been moved. It stands right over the spot. The one spot Meena needs to avoid at all costs. The closet is still there. But it has a new door. A solid door with a shining, brass lock.

"Wow," Reed says behind her. "This place looks completely different."

The relief in his voice is palpable.

"Let's do this," Danny says with a grin, walking over to the far left corner and dropping his crate of CDs on the floor. He makes a wide arc around the Ping-Pong table on the way.

Meena smiles. The pall is gone. Everyone is so relieved, it's like someone has filled the basement with happy gas. Jane picks up the remote and turns the TV to MTV2, filling the room with Weezer as Cori sets up the stereo equipment. Danny dumps out a bag filled with chips, pretzels, and candy on an old and empty bar that stands along one wall, then joins Cori. Karyn starts to pull apart the plastic bowls and cups Mrs. Davis has left them. Jeremy and Reed begin to unpack the decorations onto the couch.

Watching them work, Meena suddenly feels giddy with excitement. She says a mental thank-you to Peter's parents for refinishing the basement and walks over to help Jane and Karyn. This is perfect. There's no way Peter can be depressed in the face of all this optimistic excitement. Even she feels lighter than she has since that excruciating interview at the police station Wednesday. This is, without a doubt, one of the better ideas she's ever had.

• • •

Jeremy stands in the middle of the room with Reed, at a loss. He's been here five minutes and it already seems like everything's getting done. Which leaves him nothing but unoccupied time to think. About Josh. About tonight. About the fact that he's as nervous as he possibly can be even though it is not, technically, a date.

He glances at Reed, who's periodically glancing over at Karyn as she fills a bowl with potato chips. From the look on Reed's face, he might as well be watching a documentary about the clubbing deaths of baby seals. Jeremy sighs. He and his best friend have serious romance problems.

"Let's move the furniture," Jeremy says, clapping his hands together.

Reed looks down at the couch next to him and his eyes brighten. He's glad to have a task. "Yeah," he says.

They crouch at either end of the couch and hoist it up, then start moving toward the far wall. "So . . . Josh is coming tonight," Jeremy says.

There's a pause. Reed's eyes flick toward Jeremy. Suddenly Jeremy's heart falls. Is it possible that, after all this time and everything they've been through, Reed isn't actually comfortable with the idea of Jeremy dating a guy?

Not that it's a date . . .

"That's great," Reed says flatly as they lower the couch against the wall. "Really."

"What?" Jeremy asks, straightening up and feeling the flush in his face from lifting the couch darken into the beginnings of embarrassed anger.

"Nothing!" Reed says, hearing the confrontational quality in Jeremy's voice. "No, I really think it's great. I'm just . . ." He glances over his shoulder, lowers his voice. "Jane has a date meeting her here later, Danny has a date, you have a date. . . ."

"And there you are in the friend zone with Karyn," Jeremy finishes, feeling guilty for suspecting Reed of anything like uncharitable thoughts. He rubs his hands together, trying to smooth the red marks left in his palms from lifting the furniture.

"Exactly," Reed says. He plops down onto the couch, pushing the streamers and bags of balloons aside. He rests his elbow on the armrest and brings his fist to his temple. "It's just . . . I was *so close*, you know?"

"I know," Jeremy says, perching on the opposite armrest. He reaches up and moves the clasp on his chain away from the gold number three to the back of his neck. "This isn't a date for me, either," he says with a one-shouldered shrug. "Josh thinks we should just be friends."

"Yeah?" Reed asks, then chuckles at the pleased note in his voice. Jeremy laughs as well. He understands. He's glad they're in the same boat, too. "Sorry," Reed says. "Let's just say I've heard that one before."

"Don't worry about it," Jeremy tells him.

Sliding onto the couch on the other side of the decoration pile, Jeremy slumps down until his head is pressed into the cushion. Looks past his legs across the room at the blank wall next to the staircase. Tries not to let his eyes travel toward the closet.

"The thing is . . ." He pauses, trying to figure out how to say what he's thinking without sounding like a girl. "The thing is, just because Josh and I are friends now, that doesn't mean we'll always just be friends, you know?"

Reed takes a deep breath and looks toward the bar again, then quickly up at the ceiling. He's obviously trying to train himself to stop acting like a forlorn puppy.

"I know what you mean," he says. "She said she just needs some time, so . . . there's always a chance."

"Exactly," Jeremy says with a nod. "Don't give up yet. It's only been a couple of days. If it's meant to be, it's meant to be."

Reed cracks up laughing and Jeremy looks at him. "What?" he asks.

"You're such a freakin' sap, man," Reed says through his laughter.

Jeremy rolls his eyes and pushes himself up off the couch. "Come on, loser," he says. "We have more furniture to move."

• • •

Karyn's balling up a foil chip bag when the sound of Reed and Jeremy laughing distracts her. Her pulse races nervously as she launches the ball toward a brown paper bag she, Jane, and Meena have been using for garbage. It lands three feet to the left of the mark.

"Nice shot," Jane says from above.

She's standing on one of two folding chairs they'd found against the wall, holding up one end of a home-made Happy Birthday sign she and Karyn had made after baking the day before. Meena holds up the other end, a thumbtack pressed between her teeth.

"Iv ip stwait?" Meena asks, looking down at Karyn.

"Yeah, it's straight," Karyn replies distractedly, glancing over her shoulder as Reed and Jeremy lift an armchair and bring it over to the wall.

She feels like there's some kind of invisible force trying to pull her heart out. This isn't right. She and Reed have barely spoken since they got here. What about the whole friends thing? Was that just wishful thinking? Is it impossible for them to stay friends after everything that has happened?

"Meena, how are Peter's parents going to get him to come downstairs?" Jane asks.

"His mother couldn't think of a believable reason to get him down here, so we're gonna have to surprise him up-stairs when they come in," Meena says, shrugging. "Then he'll just take the lift thing down."

"That makes sense," Karyn says absently, looking away

from Reed the second he starts to turn his head in her direction.

Jane jumps down off her chair, picks up a roll of blue streamers, and slaps them into Karyn's hand.

"Streamer time?" Karyn asks with a sigh.

"I was thinking you and Reed could work on that side of the room," Jane says, lifting her chin toward the guys.

Karyn glances at Jane, her nerves sizzling. "Jane—"

"It's the perfect icebreaker," Jane says seriously. "You know you want to. Besides, the rest of the stuff is over there, so you'll have to cross the room at some point."

"Here's some tape," Meena says, handing her the dispenser.

"All right. Fine," Karyn replies, rolling her eyes at them and half wishing she'd never told Jane about the Reed situation. "Wish me luck."

The walk across the smallish room is impossibly long. Karyn keeps waiting for Reed to see her approaching and to make a run for it. But he and Jeremy are so busy discussing football strategy, they don't even see her until she's right in front of their faces.

"Anyone want to help me hang these things?" Karyn asks, holding up the roll of streamers and feeling like the queen of unsubtle.

"I gotta go get some CDs out of my car," Jeremy says. He shoots Reed a bolstering look, then turns and heads for the stairs.

And the king of unsubtle is . . .

"So, I guess it's you and me," Reed says, taking the streamers from her.

He smiles. It's not forced or strained or angry or false. It's just a smile. Something has changed in him since they'd arrived earlier. Since he had trouble even looking at her. Karyn wonders what Jeremy said to him. She starts to relax.

"Want to start in this corner?" Reed asks, stepping up onto the arm of the couch.

"Careful," Karyn says.

"Eh. Don't worry about me," Reed tells her, holding the streamer up to the ceiling. "Tape?"

Karyn tears off a piece of Scotch tape and holds it up to him. She can't believe how comfortable this feels. How fast she's just gone from terrified to totally fine. For the first time since their big talk in the car, she actually feels like everything is normal with Reed. It's fabulous.

And almost disappointing. Is this really possible? After the kissing and the talking and the heart breaking, everything can go back to normal this easily? It doesn't seem right.

Be grateful, Karyn tells herself as Reed climbs down again. *At least he's talking to you.*

"So . . . T. J. hates me," Reed says, starting to walk along the wall with a trail of streamer growing behind him as he carefully unrolls it.

Karyn's stomach turns and a chill rushes over her body.

141

Did Reed finally tell T. J. what happened between them? "Because of me?" she squeaks out.

"He doesn't even know about you," Reed tells her with a wry chuckle. As if he's trying to convey that if T. J. *did* know about Karyn and Reed, then Reed wouldn't be standing here to tell the tale.

"Oh. That's good," Karyn replies. *Thank God.* T. J. hates her enough as it is. If she can keep him from finding out that she'd hooked up with his brother one week after breaking up with him, things will be much easier. "So it's the football thing."

"Yeah," Reed tells her, stopping at the corner. He climbs up onto a wooden chair and twists the streamer, letting out some slack so it drapes well. "He's dropping out."

Karyn's heart falls through her boots. "Dropping out?" she repeats, shaken. "But . . . he loves it there."

"Does he?" Reed asks, looking down at her. "I mean, besides football, does he really like it there?"

"Yeah," Karyn says, confused. How can Reed not know this? "I mean, you know he loves his roommate and . . . I don't know . . . he likes going to class and doing well and feeling . . . studious, I guess."

Reed laughs and she shoots him a serious look. "Sorry," he says. "I guess I just have a hard time imagining T. J. enjoying class."

Karyn sighs, lowering herself onto the edge of the chair Reed is standing on, her back to him. "But he does, Reed," she says, resting her elbows on her knees and her chin in her hands. "He's doing pretty well, did you know that? He's getting all B's and C's."

"You're kidding me," Reed says.

He jumps down to the floor and sits on the other edge of the chair. Their arms brush against each other and their legs touch. A ticklish skitter races over Karyn's skin. Totally exciting. Totally incongruous to the conversation.

"Have you tried to talk him out of it?" Karyn asks, shifting slightly in an attempt to alleviate some of the touching—it only forces her hip closer to his.

Reed sighs. Turns his knees away so that they're almost back to back. "I would, but we're not exactly talking," he says, twirling the roll of streamers between two fingers until it's unraveled so far, there's a pile of blue at his feet. "Except to fight. We had this huge blowout and he said some things and I said some things back. . . . It was ugly."

Karyn stands up and Reed slides over, taking up the whole seat of the chair. He looks up at her and Karyn can see the pain in his eyes. She wants to reach out and hug him, but more contact at this point is not the best idea.

"I'm sure you were both just blowing off steam," she says, taking a tiny step back and hoping it's not too obvious. "You have to try to talk to him, Reed. I know he's stubborn, but he can't drop out. You can't let him."

"I know," Reed says. He bends to place the streamers on the floor, then pulls off his baseball cap and runs his hand over his hair. He looks Karyn in the eye and she knows what he's going to ask moments before he says it. "You still care about him, don't you?"

Karyn's heart catches. She knows she has to say the exact right thing here or this little normalcy between her and Reed will be over before she has the chance to appreciate it. But all she can really tell him is the truth.

"Yeah, I do," she says. He looks away, blotches of red appearing on his pale skin. "But not the way I care about you," she says, crouching in front of him, careful to keep her balance so she won't have to grab his knees for support. "And I know you guys are close. You don't want to let this go or . . . it could be really awful, Reed."

He sighs and looks at the floor. Nods. Puts his baseball cap back on. "You're right. I know." He looks across the room and Karyn wants to scream.

Look at me! Don't do this! You can still look at me!

"I'll talk to him again," he says. "But if he rips my face off, it's on your head," he adds jokingly.

And then he does look at her again. And his blue eyes are dancing. There's still sorrow and uncertainty there, but there's also still a bit of happiness. He's still the Reed she knows and loves.

"I'll take full responsibility and shoulder all costs for face replacement surgery," she says.

"Sounds fair," Reed replies. "Come on. Let's get back to the streamers."

Karyn smiles as Reed stands and climbs onto the chair again. She hands the streamers up to him and he tears off a new strand. As she watches him work, she can't help feeling kind of proud of herself. Here she is, dispensing advice to Reed about T. J. Hanging with him. Talking to him as if everything is normal. She hasn't caved to her emotions. And she feels so . . . mature.

"Thanks for telling me about his grades and everything," Reed says, jumping down again and starting across the back of the room. "I had no idea."

"I'm glad I could help," Karyn says, pulling the chair behind her.

And she's glad they talked about this. Because it's made her realize again that she's made the right decision about her and Reed. It's the right decision for all of them. But most important, for *her*.

• • •

This is the last time I'll ever turn onto my street, Peter thinks, feeling completely detached.

He watches the streetlamps go by, passes the drain down which he lost his plastic aircraft carrier when he was six, slides by the house that weird kid Stan used to live in when Peter was little.

He fiddles with the electric lock on the back door of the car. Click, click, click, click. His parents hate it. Yet they say nothing. Click, click, click, click.

His mother clears her throat. "That was a very nice

dinner," she says from the front seat. "Didn't you think that place was great, Peter?"

She looks back at him. Her expression of glee is so forced, she could be a circus clown. She's been wearing it all night, except for a brief moment when she caught sight of his appearance before they left for dinner. He wasn't exactly in the mood to shave and dress up for an occasion like this.

"Yeah, Mom," Peter says. "It was really nice. Thanks."

Her grin, impossibly, widens, and she sits straight again, satisfied with his answer.

This is the last time I'll ever pull into my driveway, Peter thinks.

He looks out across the lawn where he used to play catch with his father, glances at the loose rock along the pathway that hides all those creepy grub bugs, looks at the bushes he crashed into the first time he tried to ride a two-wheeler and realized no one ever told him how to stop.

His father cuts the engine. Gets out and helps Peter out of the car.

This is the last time I'll ever touch my father, Peter thinks, grasping his dad's arms a little more tightly than necessary as he maneuvers him into his chair. He inhales his father's crisp, clean scent, notices the cut under his chin from his razor, sees, for the first time, the tiny kinky gray hairs just above his ears.

"I bet you can't guess what we got you," his mother says as she walks behind him and his father up the ramp to the front door.

"I don't really need any presents," Peter says.

He doesn't really need much of anything. He reaches into his wheelchair pocket. The gun is still there. The gun is all he needs.

This is the last time I'm ever going to go inside my house, he thinks.

His mother smiles down at him as his father pauses and fumbles with his keys.

This is the last time I'm ever going to see my mother smile.

The heaviness in Peter's heart is almost unbearable. He just wants to get inside. Get inside. Get to his room. Get it over with. He wishes he could stop his brain from noticing these things. Seeing every detail of his life in sharp, shining Technicolor. But it won't stop. His life isn't flashing before his eyes. It's rolling by in slow motion.

The last time I'll hear the Richardsons' TV playing too loud from next door.

The last time I'll see that chip out of the molding around the door from the day my dad moved out the basement furniture.

The last time I'll ever feel my mother's hand on my back.

The last time I'll ever be pushed through the front door and into the entryway.

The last time I'll ever hear—

The lights flick on.

"SURPRISE!!!"

Peter's heart hits his throat. This can't be happening.

CHAPTER NiNE

No! Nononononononononono! Peter closes his eyes so tightly, his eyeballs hurt. But even through his eyelids, he can still feel people pressing closer.

They're laughing, clapping . . . laughing. Squealing, screaming, whispering. His mother leans close to his ear to be heard through the noise, the pumping beat of music coming up through the floorboards.

"Are you surprised?" she asks.

He doesn't answer. Doesn't move. Can't. His mother seems to take this as an answer in the affirmative and kisses him on the cheek. He can't remember the last time his mother kissed him.

This will be the last time. . . .

Peter opens his eyes and sees Meena coming toward him from the edge of the small crowd. The pain in his heart at the sight of her is searing, slicing. Her smile—her real, uninhibited, excited smile is something he's never seen before. She's happy. She's here. Why is she here? Seeing her is just going to make everything so much harder.

"Happy birthday!" Meena says, grinning and reaching out to him. Reaching out, bending down, wrapping her arms around him.

She's hugging him. Hugging him after all this time of tentative touches that took all the bravery in his soul to attempt. She holds him tightly, her long hair covering his face. He tries to hold his breath, but he can't help it. He inhales her, breathes her in, lets her scent fill his senses.

Why is this happening? Why did you do this to me? One last earthly torture test . . . ?

And then she's gone and the parade begins. The parade of faces and hands and lips and arms. Everyone comes forward in his or her turn to hug him, kiss him, shake hands with him. Some don't know how, exactly, to hug a person in a chair. To get beyond the knees and the wheels and the mechanisms and get close enough to actually hug. There are embarrassed pauses, derisive chuckles, many a reddened cheek.

Stop, Peter thinks. *No. I don't want this. Stop.*

But he doesn't have the power to put it into words. Doesn't have the power to fight. That's what he's supposed to be doing right now—giving up the fight.

Karyn's kiss lands half on his lips, half on his cheek, and she giggles. Jeremy claps him on the back. Reed does the exact same thing. Danny actually gives him a noogie. Jane bends at the waist and puts her hands on her thighs to say, "Happy birthday," before hugging him. She looks like she's talking to a four-year-old.

Peter can't believe they're all here. Why would they want to be here of all places, today of all days? What are they thinking? He looks up at the beaming, happy faces as his father pushes his wheelchair through the crowd toward the kitchen. Cori Lerner, that Josh guy Jeremy fooled around with, Quinn freakin' Saunders. Max Kang, Keith Kleiner, Doug Anderson, Shaheem Dobi, Amy Santisi, Sumit Sachdeva, Karyn, Reed, Jeremy, Jane, Meena, Danny. Face after face after face. They've ruined everything. Not that they could have ever known, but they have.

He's going to have to live through this horrible re-union—this joke of a celebration—when all he wants to do is get it over with. When all he wants to do is pull the trigger.

• • •

Meena can't stop herself from smiling as she looks around at the crowded basement, lets the sounds of raucous conversation and laughter and music fill her ears. Peter is stunned. She's never seen anyone look so surprised by anything . . . ever. Even now, minutes later, he's still stunned speechless.

"He was so surprised!" Karyn trills, rushing over in a whirl of blond hair and perfume and giving Meena a quick hug. "This was a perfect idea, Meena."

"Thanks," Meena says, tucking her hands under her arms.

"I have to say, I was actually surprised when I heard you were planning this," Karyn says, surveying the room.

"Yeah?" Meena says. Not that she blames Karyn. The antisocial walking dead don't usually throw parties.

Karyn looks at Meena from the corner of her eye and Meena feels her skin start to prickle with heat. Here it comes. . . .

"How is everything with you?" Karyn asks. "I feel like we haven't talked in forever."

"We haven't," Meena says. She takes a deep breath and forces a smile in Karyn's direction. It's not that she doesn't want to talk to her, just not about this. Not now. Not yet. "I had some . . . stuff going on," she says. "But it's getting better now."

"Anything you want to talk about?" Karyn asks, her face creased with concern.

"Not at the moment," Meena says. "But someday, maybe. Thanks for asking."

"Anytime," Karyn says. "I'm here if you need me."

"Thanks," Meena says, her heart warming as she suddenly realizes how much she's missed her friends. How great it would be to get her life back. Or at least some of it.

They both smile and look back out at the party. Meena sighs a huge sigh of relief and starts to really relax. She hasn't felt at ease in a crowd since that random party at Luke's around Halloween. And she'd only relaxed that night after she'd gotten wasted. But here, nothing can touch her. She's done this great thing for this person who has become her best friend, and she couldn't be more content.

"Hey, guys," Jeremy says, crossing the room with his friend

Josh. Jeremy hands Karyn and Meena each a cup of soda. His brow is furrowed and he seems distracted—concerned.

Meena blinks up at him, wondering what he could possibly be worried about in the midst of their raging success. "What's wrong?" she asks.

"Has anyone besides me noticed that Peter doesn't look so good?" Jeremy asks, stuffing his hands into the front pockets of his jeans. He turns his back to Peter and faces Karyn so that they won't all seem to be looking at Peter at the same time.

"I don't really know the guy, but he looks like I did after I had the stomach flu for a week," Josh puts in with no trace of irony.

"Well, he *has* been absent all week," Karyn says. "Maybe he's still sick."

Meena, for the first time since they came downstairs, really studies Peter. His skin is pale and shiny and dotted with stubble, as if he hasn't shaved in a couple of days. He's wearing an army sweatshirt with a fraying collar that has a stain right under the *m* and another on the sleeve. He's slumped back in his chair, almost lifelessly, staring straight ahead at the TV, which is no longer on.

He's just surprised, that's all, a little voice in Meena's mind tells her. But as the minutes crawl by, the less able she is to believe that. Peter looks ill. He looks weak and distressed. He looks like he could use a good long shower and a cry. But what he does not seem to be is up for a party.

Maybe he really is sick, Meena thinks. But she knows that's not it. She knows he's depressed. She just hadn't realized until now how very depressed he is.

"Wouldn't his mother have called off the party if he still wasn't feeling well?" Jeremy asks.

Meena doesn't answer. She knows what's wrong. And she knows by now that Peter's mother is either ignoring it or is too blind to see it. Peter did get bad news at the doctor on Monday and he is not taking it well. Peter needs help. Not a party. Not a bunch of people being happy all up in his face.

Peter needs help. And Meena has given him the exact opposite.

• • •

"So . . . Jane Scott!" Danny says, hooking one arm around her neck and looking around the room. "This is a party. What do you think?"

"Hey!" Jane says, flushing and casting a glance at Quinn to see if he's paying attention. He simply smiles back, amused. "I've been to a party before!"

One party, she adds silently. *One really amazing party.*

She reaches out and slips her hand into Quinn's. He turns his palm and laces his fingers through hers, giving her a little squeeze and sipping his drink, looking around the room as if he's doing nothing to cause the goose bumps running up and down her arm.

I've definitely come a long way, Jane thinks. *Two parties in two weeks. A hot date. Hanging with Reed Frasier, Danny*

Chaiken, and Cori Lerner. If my parents could see me now . . .

Jane giggles at her own thoughts.

"You know what we should do?" Danny exclaims, pushing himself away from the wall and jumping in front of them, his blue eyes wide. "We should have a lip-sync contest!"

"Please!" Cori says, reaching over to the Ping-Pong table to grab a pretzel. "What are we, twelve?"

"Maybe I am," Danny jokes, lifting his chin. "Besides, I brought my video camera," he says, bringing his arm out from behind his back to show them the impossibly small device. "Do you realize the potential for blackmail?"

Cori's face brightens. "*Now* you're thinking," she says with a nod, taking the camera from him. She turns it on Reed and hits the record button. "Reed Frasier, if you were forced to perform lip sync in front of literally dozens of scrutinizing classmates, what song would you choose?"

Reed's skin darkens beneath his freckles, but he looks squarely at the camera. "Whatever song has the fewest words," he says.

Jane and Quinn laugh, then Cori turns the camera on Danny.

"Mr. Chaiken," she says in a deep voice. She holds the camera away from her and looks through the tiny screen on the viewfinder. "Your lip-sync song of choice?"

Danny brings his hand to his chin and rubs it as if he's a scholar pondering the big bang theory. "I'd have to go with Britney Spears, 'I'm a Slave 4 You,'" he says. "I have the whole heavy-breathing thing down like you would not believe."

Cori rolls her eyes behind the camera as Jane and Quinn laugh again. Then Cori turns the camera on Jane. She lifts her hands to block the lens—a knee-jerk reaction—but Quinn puts his drink down and pulls her hands down, holding them by her waist as she struggles halfheartedly to break free.

"Jane Scott? What do you dance around to alone in your bedroom at night?" Cori asks.

"Uh . . ." Jane blushes. She wishes she could be clever and funny like Danny but draws a blank. "Probably something by Janet Jackson," she says lamely. "I listen to a lot of Janet."

"Cool," Cori says.

Quinn releases Jane's arms and she reaches up to whack his shoulder as Cori turns the camera on him. Jane gets the sudden, comical mental picture of Quinn jumping around the room to some Blink 182 song and laughs, but before Cori can ask the question, Quinn cuts her off.

"Hey . . . I think there's something wrong with your friend Peter," he says, his voice thick with concern.

"What do you mean?" Jane says with a laugh, figuring he's just trying to avoid being put on the spot. But Quinn shoots her a serious look and her laugh dies in her throat.

"He looks really out of it," Quinn says. "I mean, I don't know the guy, but doesn't he look out of it?"

Cori turns the camera toward Peter, but then her face falls and she flips the viewfinder closed. She lowers the camera slowly. The five of them look across the room to where Peter is sitting, obviously not listening to Max Kang as he babbles away. Jane feels a cold skitter rush through her veins. Peter's eyes are so blank, it's eerie. He's staring straight ahead at nothing and his jaw is set. He's pale. And he seems almost catatonic.

"He's okay. He's just . . . tired," Danny says uncertainly.

They all fall silent. Jane reaches out and takes Quinn's hand again. There's something very wrong.

• • •

Go away . . . go away . . . when are you all going to go away?

Peter has lost control over his thoughts. They race ahead of him, and as much as he struggles to hold on to one of them—any of them—they keep running past him, filling his head with white noise.

Meena is so beautiful . . . don't want to be . . . why would Mom think . . . hate this smell . . . Max's voice has never been so . . . the gun is right there . . . I should just . . . get out of my face . . . I don't even know what you're—

Peter finally manages to lift his chin slightly to the left and look up at Max Kang, who is telling an animated story about something. Something having to do with a skateboard, an ice patch, and a lot of flailing and screaming. It's all too much for his senses to bear along with the racing thoughts, so he turns his head to the right.

Karyn, Jeremy, Josh, and Meena all instantly look away and try to seem like they weren't staring at him. Jeremy and Karyn laugh a little bit too hugely at something Josh has just said.

Meena gazes down at the floor, letting her hair hide her face.

What were they thinking? Why would they want to celebrate my birthday? Don't they know how much better off they'd be if I was never born? How much better off they'd be if they'd never been in this house?

Peter closes his eyes. He can't take the sight of them anymore. He doesn't understand why they're here. Don't they see how worthless he is? Don't they see the waste of space sitting in the middle of the room? All he's ever done is bring misery to everyone around him. The six of them, his parents, Harris's parents.

I'm a useless, pathetic cripple. A useless, pathetic cripple who ruins lives. I killed a person. I killed a small, innocent person.

Slowly Peter's hands stretch out and he curls his fingers around the ends of his armrests. He clutches at them, trying with all his might to hold on to his emotions. To keep from lashing out and adding yet another layer of misery to these people's lives.

But they asked for it. They're here. They're the ones who, for some reason, insist on being close to me. . . .

"Dude! Just think! This time next year, you'll be able to get up outta that chair and dance on your birthday!" Max Kang says, slapping him on the back.

The room falls nearly silent. Everyone heard that. They all know it's not true. They're all pitying him. They all know he'll never be able to do anything ever again.

"Get out," Peter says through his teeth, so quietly, he can barely hear it himself.

Max's face creases. It looms above Peter like a balloon. "What?" it says, blinking.

"I said . . . *get out!*" Peter shouts at the top of his lungs. *"GET OUT!"*

He glares around the room, his eyes on fire. They're all scared. They're all pitying. They're all morons. Peter can't wait another second to be rid of them.

"Get out! All of you just get the hell out of my house!"

CHAPTER TEN

"I can't take this anymore. I can't. I can't. I don't understand why you're all here. I don't want you here. I don't want any of you. . . ."

Peter is rambling. He hears himself rambling. He sees everyone's disturbed glances as they slide by him toward the stairs, some of them keeping their distance as if they're afraid he's going to strike out at them. He knows he looks insane. He knows he sounds insane. But he's on a roll. And letting it out feels so good, he can't stop himself. It's his one last rant.

"Sorry, guys . . . sorry . . . thanks for coming," Meena says repeatedly. She's somewhere behind him . . . off to his right. Standing at the bottom of the steps.

"Why are you apologizing?" Peter mumbles, staring down at a distant spot on the floor. "Don't apologize for me. It doesn't matter. They don't care. I don't care. They don't care about me. I don't understand. . . ."

The steps are creaking under the weight of more people than they've supported in years. Peter feels every noise in his bones. He just wants them to be gone. Be gone so he can do what he has to do. He's sweating from the strain of staying quiet as long as he did. From holding it all in. He rocks forward and back slightly as he talks. He'll just keep talking until they're all gone. Until they're finally gone and he can do what he has to do.

"Just leave me alone . . . leave me alone . . . leave me alone . . ."

Finally the room is mercifully quiet. No more music. No more laughter. No more voices. It's blissfully, serenely quiet. Peter falls silent. He lifts his eyes.

He is not alone.

Karyn. Jeremy. Reed. Jane. Danny. Meena.

They are against the wall. On the love seat. On the floor. He can feel Meena behind him, sitting on the bottom step. They are all here.

"You guys," Peter says in a hoarse, weak voice. "Please just go, all right?"

They look at one another. Jeremy, hands behind his back against the wall, shifts his weight from one foot to the other. Karyn wipes a tear away from her cheek and looks away. Meena takes a long, deep breath.

"No way," Reed says finally.

"Not until you tell us what's wrong," Karyn pipes in. "What is going on with you?"

Peter looks down at his hands. His heart is trying to push its way out of his chest. This is too much. This was supposed to be so simple. This was not supposed to happen.

"Maybe we can help," Jane says after a prolonged silence.

Peter scoffs. "I don't know why you would want to."

"What, are you kidding?" Danny says. "You're our friend."

"I'm not your friend," Peter says, using any and all determination left in him to stare Danny down. "I'm worthless."

Someone . . . Jeremy . . . lets out a breath.

"What are you talking about?" Meena says, her voice wet with tears.

Peter can't look at her. He refuses to turn his head. He can see enough out of the corner of his eye to know that she's hugging herself tightly. That her face is soaked.

"Peter, if it wasn't for you, I wouldn't have had anyone to talk to when my mom went psycho a couple of weeks ago," Karyn says, leaning forward in her seat.

Whatever, Peter thinks. *You would have figured it out.*

Reed shifts uncomfortably, glancing at Karyn but then focusing on Peter. "And you helped me figure out that whole thing with T. J."

Yeah. That *was a tough decision. To be a famous quarterback or not to be a famous quarterback? Real hard.*

"You were my friend when half the guys on the team stopped hanging out with me," Jeremy points out. "In case you haven't noticed, when we're in the weight room . . . we're the only people in the weight room."

So? Peter thinks. *Who needs those meatheads, anyway?*

"And you convinced me to go to that party," Jane says.

She looks at the others. "I know it sounds stupid, but it wasn't . . . not to me."

"It's not stupid," Danny says. He pushes himself away from the wall next to Jeremy and looks down at Peter. "You thinking you're worthless is stupid."

"Danny—"

"What? I'm just saying . . ."

Peter stares at his fingers, his chest filled with desperation. They don't get it. They don't get anything. They didn't need him to help them with any of those things. He thought they did, but it was all just a joke. No one needs him for anything. They'll all be much better off without him weighing them down—holding them back.

"Peter? Are you going to say anything?" Meena asks quietly.

Peter feels his eyes fill at the sound of her voice. Feels his chin quiver slightly. Holds it back. Meena. The cruelest part of the joke. The dangled carrot. The gold star. He can't believe he ever actually thought they were going to be together. That anyone as perfect as her could be meant for him. He wishes she would leave. Having her here is worse than the other five combined. Having her here is torture.

Then she moves. And for a split second, Peter thinks it's over. That she's going to turn and flee up the stairs and he'll finally be able to get this over with. But instead, she floats over to him. She crouches at his feet. She reaches out to hold the wheels on his chair.

"Are you even going to look at me?" she demands quietly,

her glittering dark eyes searching his face. "I don't think I'd be alive right now if it wasn't for you. I *know* I wouldn't."

And something inside Peter snaps.

"Shut up," he says, tears spilling onto his face.

Meena blinks and pulls back, hurt.

"Just shut up, all of you," he says, bringing a fist to his forehead. "Shut up about what a great freakin' guy I am."

He looks up at them, hovering around him—watching him like he's some kind of mental patient. His voice gains strength and volume with every word.

"I am *not* a great guy. I am *not* anyone's friend. I am nothing!" he shouts, his whole face shaking with strain, his vision blurred with tears. "And the fact that I'm never going to walk again is just fate's way of punishing me!"

Jeremy and Reed look at each other, pale. Karyn looks sick. Jane hides her face in her hands. Danny's fists clench at his sides.

"Peter—"

"No!" Peter shouts. "I killed Harris Driver right here in this room seven years ago today! Have you all just forgotten about that? I'm a murderer and I'm being punished! That's all I am! I'm being punished. . . ."

Aside from Peter's sobs, there is not a sound in the room.

• • •

It's been there all night, this unspoken thing. This horrible event hovering between them. Blanketing the room with a dark cloud that no one else could see. Now Jane can feel the cloud descending. She can feel it pressing down on her shoulders, on all of them. She's surprised they can all still manage to breathe.

Everyone is waiting for someone to speak. Her. Jane. They're all waiting for her and she knows it. She knows that she's the only one that can stop Peter's pain. She's the only one that can make those heartrending sobs stop.

He thinks it was him. He's sitting there and he's never going to walk again and he thinks it was his fault. That he's to blame.

She opens her mouth. Closes it. Opens it again. Closes it. She clears her throat. They all look at her sitting cross-legged on the floor. She clutches her knees with her hands. It's time.

"It wasn't you, it was me," she says. Just like that. Just like answering an oral test question. Simple. To the point.

"What?" Danny says, his face scrunched up with surprise.

"I don't understand why Peter thinks it was his fault," Jane says firmly, holding on to her knees for dear life. She'd hold on to anything at this point. "You all know it was me."

"Jane," Meena says, sitting her butt down hard on the floor in front of Peter's chair and turning toward her. "Don't do—"

"No, Meena, come on," Jane says. "If it wasn't for me, Harris would be alive right now. I'm the one who went snooping around down here. I'm the one who just *had* to go in the closet. Me and my stupid curiosity."

She always had to know everything. Even as a kid. She was constantly asking questions, going through her parents' things, going through other people's things. "Greedy for knowledge" is what her father used to call her with a proud spark in his eye. Always so proud of his intelligent, curious daughter.

That curiosity is what got Harris Driver killed.

Jane takes a deep breath and looks around the room. Reed's elbows are braced against his knees as he sits on the love seat, his hands flattened together like a steeple and held in front of his mouth. Karyn's elbow is on the armrest, her hand to her forehead. She can't even look at Jane. Danny's arms are wrapped around himself as he hovers above her. Jeremy's eyes are on his feet.

And Peter. Peter is looking at her like she's lost her mind. Maybe she has. But it's about time.

"Me and my stupid curiosity got Harris killed, Peter," Jane says, her heart turning in her chest. "It wasn't you."

• • •

"She's right, Peter, it wasn't you," Meena says, clutching her hands together as she stares down at the carpet. She finally manages to lift her eyes and look at Jane. "But it wasn't you, either."

"Thank you!" Reed says, lifting a hand and then slumping back into the love seat as if he let out all the air in his body with that one exclamation.

Meena's face heats up and she finds herself looking at the blue carpeting again. "It was me."

"No, it wasn't," Jane says.

"Yes. It was," Meena replies.

Suddenly her whole body is itching to let it out. To tell

the truth, after all this time. The last secret she'd confessed had only tortured her for about six weeks, but this one . . . this one has haunted her for years. All this time, she'd let her parents keep calling her their little baby. Treating her like she was something precious and pure. And all this time, she's the only one who has known what she really is.

Until now.

"We both went in that closet, Jane, but I was the one who needed to go through everything," Meena says. "All those family photo boxes . . . I was the one who wanted to look for pictures of Peter. You were ready to bag the whole thing."

She risks a glance at Jane, who opens her mouth, furrows her brow, and says nothing. Because she knows. She's realizing Meena is right. All the little hairs on Meena's arms stand on end.

"I'm the one who found the gun. I'm the one who took it out," Meena says. "If I had just left it there, Harris never would have—"

"No," Jeremy says suddenly, startling Meena. Everyone turns to look at him, standing against the wall next to the television. His hands are behind his back and he pushes himself away from the wall. "You're remembering it all wrong," he says. "You both are."

• • •

Jeremy's talking, but he can't believe it. He can't believe that after those endless, torturous years, he's just letting it spill like it's nothing. Just letting it all come out. But he's had a taste of how liberating it is to tell the truth about himself. And he's not going to let Jane and Meena feel guilty about something they had no part in.

"Harris is dead because of me," Jeremy says, looking down at Meena and Jane. "You guys were going to put it back, remember? Yeah, you found it, but you knew it was wrong to take it out and you would have put it back . . . if it wasn't for me."

Meena and Jane exchange a glance and Jeremy knows that they're remembering it now. Knows that they're agreeing with him.

"I walked in on you, remember?" Jeremy continues. "I made you give me the gun." He looks around at the rest of them apologetically, but Karyn is staring off into space and Reed is rubbing his face with his hands. "I'd never seen one in person. . . . I wanted to see how heavy it was. I remember thinking . . . I remember thinking about freakin' Harrison Ford."

He laughs at himself. He was so stupid. He thought he was being cool. He'd been watching all the old *Star Wars* and *Indiana Jones* movies with his father. Jeremy had loved those times with his dad, sitting on the couch, watching his father's favorites. One of the moments his dad loved the best was when Indiana Jones was being impressively threatened by a guy with a samurai sword and, nonchalant, Jones whips out a gun and shoots the guy cold.

Jeremy had wanted to act that moment out. Could

imagine his father looking on, laughing. Could imagine the pride in his dad's eyes. It's always been about being the perfect son. Making his father proud.

"If it hadn't been for me, that gun would have stayed in the closet where it belonged," Jeremy says.

"Yeah, but if it wasn't for me, it never would have been loaded," Danny says bluntly.

"What?" Jeremy asks.

"Nice try, Mandile . . . we have some lovely parting gifts for you, but you are not tonight's winner," Danny says with a sarcastic edge.

• • •

Danny's hands are stuffed under his arms and he pinches at the flesh on his sides, each pang of pain bringing more tears to his eyes. He once did this to try to make himself feel something when he was in one of his foggy dazes, but now it's just habit. He doesn't need help feeling anything at this moment. He's feeling it all. Despair, guilt, relief, disbelief, fear. No drug could dull the concoction of emotion that flows through his heart as he looks around at each of their faces.

They all think it's their fault. How can six people be so monumentally stupid?

"I loaded the gun, you guys. Me." He shakes his head and kicks his toe into the carpet over and over and over again. "You can't kill someone without bullets."

Reed's voice is muffled through his hands. "Yeah, but—"

"I was all obsessed with *Unforgiven* and *Tombstone,* remember?" Danny says, shaking his head at himself. "I actually used to bring that dumb ass cap gun to school. They confiscated it in gym once and I had a fit."

"I remember that," Jane says flatly.

Danny snorts. He was a basket case even then. Maybe if they'd started medicating him sooner . . .

God, is that why I did it? Danny wonders, his stomach in knots. *Was I manic that day?*

But he's gotten off track.

"*I* took the gun from Jeremy. *I* went back to the closet to find the bullets. *I* loaded the thing," Danny says, staring at whoever will look at him in the eye—Meena, Jane, Jeremy. "I thought I was all Eastwood, spinning the barrel, aiming at that old, crappy dartboard they had on the wall." He gestures over his shoulder to the spot where the board once hung. "You guys may all think it was your fault, but Harris wouldn't have died if I hadn't broken out the bullets. You've gotta—"

"Enough!"

There's an audible gasp as everyone turns to look at Reed. The sheer volume of his voice shocks Danny silent. Reed's blue eyes are glistening from all the unshed tears. He pushes himself up from the love seat.

"I can't take this anymore," he says, glaring at Danny, the veins in his neck pulsating under his skin. "Maybe you loaded it, okay? But I'm the asshole who pulled the trigger."

● ● ●

"I don't get it. I really don't. I don't understand you guys," Reed says, pacing back and forth in front of Peter.

Tears slip down his cheeks as he shakes his head and tries to get a grip on everything he's just heard. All this time he's been keeping his mouth shut about his father. Watching how the silence ate away at his family. But little did he know that keeping his mouth shut about something else was eating away at five innocent people. Reed's heart is being ripped into a thousand pieces. All this time Peter, Jane, Meena, Jeremy, Danny—they've all thought it was them. And if he'd just opened his mouth, they wouldn't have had to live with that.

"I'm so sorry," Reed says, finally stopping and sitting on the love seat again. He buries his face in his hands. "I'm so sorry I put you guys through this."

Karyn's hand is on his back. He doesn't deserve her. Not even her touch. He pulls away.

"Reed, what are you talking about?" Karyn says.

"It was my fault. All of it," Reed says, looking up. "I took the gun from Danny and I pointed it at the dartboard and *I pulled the trigger*. Don't you remember?"

It's all so clear and vivid in his mind, it seems impossible that anyone else could have forgotten.

"Yeah, but nothing happened," Danny says finally. "There was no bullet."

"Yeah, but if I hadn't pulled that trigger, the bullet that killed Harris wouldn't have advanced into the chamber," Reed says matter-of-factly. He looks down at his hands. "I don't know what I was thinking. I knew it was wrong."

You were thinking about Dad, a little voice in his head reminds him. *You were imagining what his face would look like if you pulled a gun on him. You wanted him to feel as scared as you and T. J. always felt.*

A fat tear falls from Reed's eye and plops to the rug in front of him. He sniffles. He looks up at Jane.

"You asked me to put it away after that," he says. "You were scared. Remember?"

Jane's brow furrows. Clearly she's trying. Trying to recall this detail that Reed remembers so well.

"I do," Karyn says, her voice unnaturally husky. "I remember. I remember that Jane wanted to put it away, but I grabbed it from you. I called her a wuss and I took the gun and Peter and I kept playing."

Reed looks at Karyn as she starts to cry, her body racked with sobs, her skin blotchy. Not her. Not her, too.

• • •

"You would have put it away, but I took it," Karyn says, turning her moist eyes on Reed. "And Peter and I . . . we took turns, you know? Twirling it and pretending we had holsters and whatever."

Peter's hands reach out and grip his armrests. He's remembering, but she knows he's remembering it wrong. He's remembering that he did it, but he didn't. He did nothing wrong.

"At one point, Peter wouldn't give it back to me, so I tried to grab it, and we ended up wrestling for it," Karyn says, struggling to talk through her tears. "And then . . . then Harris came over and he . . ."

Karyn's sobs take over. She remembers exactly what Harris looked like that day. His big brown curls. His even bigger brown eyes. The blue-and-red-striped shirt that she thought was so dorky. She remembers his laugh. She hears it now as clearly as if he's sitting right next to her.

"I had the gun," she says finally, trying to catch her breath. "It fell out of my hand. It slipped . . . and it went off."

She stops and looks across the room to where the Ping-Pong table now sits. The Davises must have wanted to cover the space. Make it harder to envision the little boy's body there, on the floor, covered in blood. But Karyn can remember it. She sees it all the time in her dreams.

His eyes open. His little hands in fists. He looked . . . surprised.

"And we all lied," Karyn says, her bottom eyelids full of tears. "We blamed it on him. We told Peter's dad and the police that Harris had found the gun. That Harris had dropped it. That Harris had basically killed himself."

She takes a deep breath, looks around the room at her friends. "You all lied . . . for me."

CHAPTER ELEVEN

Peter is holding so much in, he has to hold his breath to keep it there. If he could move his legs, he'd be squirming or pacing or maybe running from the room right now. But all he can do is hold his breath. And squeeze his fingers tighter around his armrests. And sweat. And try not to cry. But it all wants to come out. The words. The tears. The air. Finally he starts to see spots in front of his eyes, and he lets it all go.

"What is *wrong* with you people!?!"

Six pairs of eyes look over at him, surprised. As if they've forgotten he's in the room. They're all so wrapped up in their personal delusions and false memories, they don't even know that he's here.

"What . . . what do you mean?" Jane asks, blinking a few times. She seems dazed. As if she's just come out of a dream.

"I *mean* you're all nuts," Peter says bluntly. "Did you even hear yourselves? None of what any of you did makes you responsible for what happened that day." He looks from face to face, incredulous. "'Oh . . . I went into the *closet*,'" he mimics, looking at Jane. "'My *curiosity* killed Harris.' 'But I'm the one who had to play Dirty Harry,'" he says, glancing at Danny. "Do you know what that makes you guys guilty of? Being kids! We were all just kids! You were doing the things kids do! You guys didn't kill Harris."

Peter looks at them. Waits for the realization to come over their faces. Waits for them to admit the truth. That they're wrong. That Peter is, in fact, the only one who did anything wrong. Meena sits up straight and looks at Reed. Reed looks at Karyn. Karyn looks at Jeremy. Jeremy looks at Danny. Danny looks at Jane. Something is passing between them. Some understanding. But Peter can't read it. He can't read their expressions.

"So . . . what the hell did *you* do?" Danny asks finally, stuffing his hands into the pockets of his beat-up cargo pants.

Their faces all turn to Peter again. Unabashed curiosity. Challenge. Expectation. They wait for him to absolve them.

Peter clears his throat and pulls his hands away from the armrests. He looks down at his fingers as he presses them together. He doesn't want to say this. Even after all this catharsis. All these supposed confessions. Even after his first outburst, he doesn't want to say it. All he wants is to end it. End everything.

"Come on, Peter. We all talked," Jeremy says, a dare in his voice.

Peter clenches his jaw, his teeth clicking together. Fine. If this is the way it's got to be—if he has to say the words before he can leave this place—then so be it.

"You know how Karyn said the gun slipped from her hands?" Peter says.

The gun. The gun is right in his pocket right now. It's been there all evening, unbeknownst to his completely oblivious parents. He doesn't have to do this. He can just end it right now.

But he won't. He won't do that to them. Not after everything he's already done. Not in front of them.

"Well, it didn't. It didn't slip. I took it," Peter says, looking at Karyn, whose face is shining with tears. "I pulled it out of your hand. I remember . . . I remember thinking, 'This is *my* birthday. This is *my* father's gun. Why should *they* get to play with it?'"

He pauses as his eyes well up and he lets out a snort of a laugh. "Can you believe it? I pulled it away and I cocked the thing, all because I was being selfish. Because I couldn't share. And when I dropped it, Harris died. I only had it away from you for a second, Karyn, but it was me, not you."

He stops and pulls in a breath that breaks a few times over the lump in his throat. "God, he wouldn't have even *been* here if he hadn't wanted to give me this present I'd been hinting about nonstop for a month. It wasn't any of you. It was me. I'm to blame."

There. It's done. Now they can all just go and let him get on with it. Let him put himself out of this misery. Let him give Harris and his family the justice they deserve.

"Peter."

It's Meena's voice. It cuts right through him.

Don't talk to me. Not you. Not you. Not you.

"Peter, are *you* even hearing *your*self?" Meena asks. She pushes herself onto her knees. Rests her delicate hands on his lifeless legs. Looks up into his stinging eyes.

"What you just said . . . what you said about us all being kids and just doing what kids do . . . doesn't the same apply to you?" she asks, her dark eyes almost serene.

"No," Peter blurts out.

"Why not?" Reed says, sitting forward in his seat.

"Because," Peter answers, shooting him a glare.

"But Peter . . . you just said you tried to get the gun from Karyn because you were being selfish," Meena continues. "A selfish little kid. Isn't that what little kids are? You wanted your toy back—your dad's gun—and so you took it."

"You were never very good at sharing," Jane says with a hint of sarcasm.

"See?" Meena says, her lips lifting into the tiniest of smiles. "You were just a kid. You were just playing like the rest of us. And so what if you wanted some stupid present so badly that Harris was psyched to give it to you? We all did that before birthdays—running around telling everyone to get us this game or that doll or this book."

Meena, still holding on to Peter, turns and looks at the others, all of whom seem to be absorbing these words—letting it in—letting it wash through them. "Harris died, but it wasn't our fault. It wasn't any of our faults. It was all just an accident.

An accident that killed someone, but still an accident."

Peter's chest is so full, it hurts. He feels a part of him . . . a part buried deep, deep down, trying to pull its way out— wanting to believe what Meena is saying.

We were just playing. . . . We were all just kids. . . .

When Peter tries to breathe again, the air catches up in his throat and the tears in his eyes spring forth. He brings his hand to his face and leans his elbow on the armrest, looking away from them all. Looking over at the empty stairs.

Can it really be . . . ? No . . . it was me. . . . But what if it wasn't? What if it just happened? What if Meena is right?

Silent tears rush down Peter's face, dropping onto his sweatshirt, wetting his neck. Everything hurts so much. The dull ache he's felt for so long seems to be intensifying, throbbing, pinching. It's trying to force its way out. Trying to push out with the tears. But how can he do it? How can he let go of the pain and guilt that has been with him for so long? It's like trying to suddenly believe that some fundamental truth is just not so. Like the sky is not blue or that Monday doesn't come after Sunday.

"And Peter . . . look how much you've done since the day Harris died," Meena says, leaning to her left, trying to get him to look at her. "Look at how much you've helped all of us. You didn't have to, but you did. And we're all here now, together for the first time since . . . since it happened."

Peter looks at her from the corner of his eye.

"That's because of you," she says. "We're all here . . . for you."

Finally Peter can't take it anymore. If she's right—if it's true—then maybe he isn't in this chair as a punishment. Maybe his accident was just that—an accident. Maybe God isn't telling him he's worthless.

Maybe he doesn't deserve to die.

He brings both hands to his face and starts to cry for real—letting it all out—the pain, the guilt, the loud, racking sobs that are choking him. He lets them out into the quiet room. He knows they're all watching him, but he doesn't care.

Nothing has ever felt this way before. As it comes out of him, pushes out of him, everything inside him changes. The longer he cries, the more he feels it. He feels warm . . . new . . . cleansed.

After a moment, a few moments, an hour, he has no idea, Peter exhausts himself. When he wipes his face dry and looks out at the room again, they're all still here. Reed's eyes are wet. Karyn is still sobbing quietly. Jeremy presses the heel of his hand into his eye and sniffles. But other than that, no one has moved. No one has fled. They're all simply waiting for him.

Shaking, Peter reaches down into the pocket on his wheelchair and pulls out the gun.

Meena falls back. Jane lets out a gasp. Reed sits forward so quickly, Peter flinches from the movement.

"What is this, a reenactment?" Danny cracks, the tense vibe in his tone betraying the joke.

Peter turns the gun. He releases the barrel. He lets all the bullets slide out into his lap with an oddly pleasant tinkling sound.

"No," Peter answers, placing the gun in his lap next to the little pile of ammunition. "No one is going to die tonight."

And as he says it, a long, slow grin stretches its way across his face. It's true. No one is going to die. He's going to live.

"What was it doing in there, man?" Jeremy asks. He has his hands pressed into the sides of his head as if he'd started to run his fingers through his hair and they'd gotten stuck there.

"Let's just say that no one in this room is responsible for taking Harris's life, but you're all responsible for saving mine," Peter says.

In a rush of breath and movement, Meena is suddenly in Peter's arms. She's hugging him so tightly, he can feel his shoulder blades coming closer together. He closes his eyes, reaches up, and holds her. Everyone else in the room is moving for the first time in a long time. He can hear them shifting, whispering. Someone lets out a tense laugh. But Peter won't open his eyes. Won't move. And from the way Meena is holding him, she's not budging anytime soon.

I can't believe I almost gave this up, Peter thinks, his heart feeling something close to light for the first time in years. *I can't believe I almost gave up on life.*

• • •

Reed takes the stairs to T. J.'s room two at a time. His body is bursting with unspent energy. All those emotions swirling back at Peter's—all the letting go and being truthful and feeling free—has combined to make Reed both exhausted and incredibly hyper at the same time. But the one thing that's clear is that anything is possible. If, on the same night, seven people can be absolved of the crime that's been keeping them miserable for seven years, anything can happen.

He pounds on the door to T. J.'s room. Takes a step back. Can't wait for it to open. Opens it himself.

T. J. is lying on his side on his bed. He looks up from the *ESPN* magazine he's reading and his eyes are stone-cold. "I didn't answer for a reason," he says.

"I don't care," Reed answers, grinning.

T. J. shakes his head and looks back down at his magazine. He obviously doesn't want to talk. But he obviously doesn't feel like fighting, either. Reed sees that as a point in his favor.

"Look, I only came in here because I realized that there's something I've never said to you, and it needs saying," Reed tells the top of his brother's head.

"Oh yeah?" T. J. says, turning the page listlessly. Totally disinterested. "What's that?"

"Thank you," Reed says.

T. J. looks up at Reed, sits up straight, and lays the magazine aside. "Okay, I'll bite. Thank you for what? Sucking so much, the BC people want to throw me over?"

"No," Reed says. "Thank you for protecting me from Dad. All I've done my entire life is try to make it up to you, but I just realized tonight that I've never said thank you. So . . . thank you."

"Thank you," T. J. replies flatly. He glances away and takes a deep breath, slowly shaking his head. "I don't know what to say."

"Say you won't drop out of school," Reed says, crossing his arms over his chest. His heart is pounding a mile a minute and he feels like he could run a cross-country race right now. He has to hold on to himself to keep himself from bouncing frenetically around the room.

"Come again?" T. J. says, raising his eyebrows.

"In case you haven't noticed, you've been doing well at school," Reed says. "And college isn't just about football. And football isn't the only future . . . for either of us."

Reed walks across the room and back again, finally giving in to his need to move. "Besides, I know I'll play a lot better next year if you're there."

T. J. gives a sarcastic laugh and looks down at the green throw rug dotted with little footballs. "I don't know, man," he says, cocking his head. "I don't know if I can stand on the sidelines and watch you play."

Reed's heart gives an extra, pained thump and he pauses in his pacing. "Come on, T. J., think about it. The Frasier brothers back together again."

T. J. pushes himself off his bed and walks over to the far

wall, rubbing his face with his hand. His whole body seems to be coiled with tension as he stares at the wall. At nothing. "Do you have any idea how humiliating that would be?"

"It doesn't have to be," Reed says. "It's only humiliating if you let it be. But if you stay . . . if you stay, you're being the bigger man, right? You're not letting your little brother chase you out."

Slowly T. J. turns to face Reed. He levels Reed with a stare, but it's not an angry stare. It's a contemplative stare.

"But what would I say to the team?" T. J. asks.

"Tell them . . . I don't know . . . tell them I'm a lucky son of a bitch," Reed says, throwing his hands up. Then he has an idea. Something he can say that will get T. J. to stay. A challenge. "Tell them you're just biding your time until you win the spot back. And that meanwhile, you're going to go after a new starting position of your own. Jack Torren's been a little off his game lately, right? You know you could make a great running back. . . ."

Suddenly T. J.'s eyes brighten. He slowly moves his hand away from his face and smiles, lifting his chin. "Interesting," he says, the first promising hint of possibility in his voice. "Yeah, Coach has been upset with Jack. And I'm definitely faster than him."

T. J. leans over and picks up his old, battered football off his bed. He whacks it against Reed's chest and Reed reaches up to cradle it, still grinning.

"So maybe I'll go for running back," T. J. says. "But

you better watch your back, little bro," he adds. "I'm gonna be on your heels every step of the way."

Reed tosses the ball up into the air and T. J. catches it. "I'm counting on it."

• • •

"Anyone mind if I pass out in my hot chocolate?" Karyn asks, her head tipping forward slightly. She left Peter's house less than fifteen minutes ago with Danny, Jane, and Jeremy and headed for the diner. It had seemed like a good idea at the time, but now she's so tired, she can feel every single muscle in her back for the first time in her life and they're all aching.

"Not a problem," Danny replies, whipping out his camera. "But I get to sell the tape."

Everyone laughs quietly and then lapses into silence once again. Karyn looks across the speckled diner table at Jeremy and Jane, both of whom look as wiped as she feels. But it's a good kind of wiped—the kind she gets after a long, satisfying workout. She's drained, but she's happy in the knowledge that the guilt is gone for good. It's all surprisingly over.

"So . . . what did you tell Quinn when you called him?" Karyn asks, stirring her drink and watching the little marshmallows turn into white swirls.

"An abbreviated version of the truth," Jane replies with a shrug. "He understood why I wanted to call the night short, but I'm sure he's going to want all the details in the morning."

"Yeah, Cori was pretty curious," Danny says, pulling the little cup of sugar cubes over to him and starting a pyramid of the tiny blocks in the center of the table. "She moved here after the whole Harris thing and she had no idea I was even there when it happened."

Jeremy laughs. "It's weird, isn't it? To think that there are some people who don't even know?" he says.

"What's weird is talking about it at all," Karyn says, scrunching up her nose. "I mean, after all this time of working so hard to avoid the subject."

"Yeah," Jane says, staring at some random spot on the table. "Weird."

The door swings open and Reed walks in. Karyn's heart leaps at the sight of him. He's clearly tired, but smiling. When he'd said he was going to go home to talk to T. J., Karyn wasn't quite sure how it was going to go. But from the look on Reed's face, it couldn't have gone too badly.

"Everything okay?" Karyn asks, scrooching over and pressing Danny closer to the wall.

Reed sits down next to her and plucks the top cube off Danny's pyramid, causing the whole thing to crumble.

"Hey!" Danny says indignantly.

Reed pops the sugar cube into his mouth and rolls it around. "I think it's going to be, yeah," he says. Karyn's heart warms a bit as he smiles at her, then looks away.

"So," Jeremy says, after draining the last of his soda. "What do we do now?"

They all look at one another for a beat, and Karyn's

mind is a complete blank. It's like it's spent the last couple of hours being so entirely full, it can't even process a simple question anymore. All she knows is she's feeling airy and happy and seriously sleepy.

"I propose a pact," Danny says finally, lifting his chocolate shake. Everyone lifts their glasses and mugs and waits. "I propose that we never . . . *ever* . . . try to do anything on December seventh *ever* again."

Karyn laughs along with the others. "I'm in!" she says.

They all clink glasses, then drink—Jeremy crunching on ice cubes. Karyn leans back in her seat and almost instantly feels her eyes start to close.

"Of course, we're going to have to get Peter to officially change his birthday," Jeremy says.

"Maybe we should suggest a nice balmy day in June," Jane puts in.

"What happened to Meena and Peter, anyway?" Reed asks, picking up his tiny water glass again and taking a sip. "Are they okay?"

Jeremy shrugs and glances at Karyn and she tilts her head. "Who knows?" she says.

"I hope they are," Jane says, toying with her fork and knife.

"I think they will be," Jeremy puts in hopefully.

Karyn smiles and sees that the rest of them are smiling, too. Peter and Meena are going to be okay. It feels true. It feels right. She looks at Reed and he's already watching her. She holds his gaze for a long moment, letting his confidence and love fill her.

For the first time in a long while she knows for certain that they're all going to be okay.

• • •

Peter has never experienced a night as silent as this one. There are no cars on his street. No stereos. No planes overhead. Even the Richardsons' TV is mute. All he can hear is his breathing. Meena's breathing. The hushed, calm thoughts floating through his mind. Meena pushes her feet into the porch floor and the swing they sit on creaks back, then forward.

Peter shifts his arms under the blanket and his hand brushes Meena's. She shivers.

"Are you cold?" Peter asks, reaching over to pull the blanket closer around Meena's shoulders.

"Nope," she answers, shaking her head. "I'm fine."

She lets out a long breath and the fog hangs in the air a moment.

"I don't know if this is the right time to bring it up, but they arrested Steven," Meena says, looking out across the yard. "I made a statement and they arrested him."

Peter's heart goes out to Meena and he wishes he could just absorb it all for her. All the pain and worry over what's to come. But he knows that he can't. All he can do is be here for her. And he's grateful that he can be. That he didn't let her down. That he didn't let despair win.

"Are you going to be okay?" he asks, turning to look at her profile.

"I think I am," she says, staring down at the fading plaid pattern on the blanket.

"Well, the doctor said that, barring a miracle, I'm never going to walk again," Peter tells her, letting the hollow feeling he gets whenever he thinks about the chair and his legs and his situation overtake him and then waiting for it to dissipate. That's the thing he'd forgotten—that it goes away. It takes a while, but he doesn't feel hollow *all* the time. Especially not when Meena's here.

"Are you going to be okay?" Meena asks, studying him now.

Peter cracks a small, sad smile. "I think I am."

Meena exhales loudly and smiles as well. "Well, there couldn't be a more messed up couple than the two of us, could there?" she says.

Peter's heart skips a beat, forcing the hollowness out completely. He couldn't have heard her right, could he? He presses his hands into the swing at his sides and turns himself slightly, causing the rickety chair to rock.

"Did you just say 'couple'?" he asks.

Meena turns her head slowly to look at him and there's more love in her eyes than he's ever seen before from anyone in his lifetime. "Yeah. I think I did," she says, blushing.

Then she blinks and the slightest cloud of uncertainty flits across her face. She looks at his mouth, then into his

187

eyes again. Peter's skin tingles. He wants to tell her she doesn't have to do it. He knows it has to be hard. But the louder voice in his head wins out—the one that wants to kiss her so badly, he can already taste it.

Meena takes a deep breath, leans in slowly. And then, her lips touch Peter's. His eyes flutter closed and he presses back, savoring the closeness, the warmth, the texture and scent of her. And then, she tentatively pulls away. Sits back in the swing. Smiles.

Peter bites his lip to keep from laughing with giddiness. It was fast. It was barely there. But it happened. His first kiss with Meena. And it melts his heart.

"So, you never got to make your birthday wish," Meena says, looking over at him through her lashes. Glowing.

He reaches over under the blanket and laces his fingers through hers. Meena squeezes his hand tightly and Peter can't believe that just earlier this evening, he was on the brink. That he hadn't been able to imagine a release from the pain. That he'd thought of himself as so entirely worthless. Feeling like this is worth everything. Making Meena smile like that is worth even more. How could he have ever thought of leaving this world? Of leaving her.

"I don't mind," Peter tells her, squeezing back. "It just came true."